Forheavenstake

FORHEAVENSTAKE

D.D. Cross

MMA

Publishing

D.D. CROSS

Copyright © 2013 by D.D. Cross

All rights reserved under International and Pan-American Copyright Conventions. Published by the MMA Publishing Group International.

ISBN-13: 978-0615760445
ISBN-10: 0615760449

Original Art by D.D. Cross

Printed in the United States of America

10 9 8 7 6 5 4 3 2 1

This is dedicated to anyone who hasn't
been dead yet

PART I

1

DEAD AGAIN

The last thing I remember was ridin' my airboat real fast. I had that sucker goin' full throttle through the swamp, hoppin' over gators, thumpadabump bumpin' the `luminum hull, and sloshin' through thick patches of mangrove and sawgrass. I could feel the spiny-edge leaves thrashin' my face and jabbin' into me. I couldn't see but for nothin', then I hear this clunk like an auto junkyard'd been nuked. It was so loud my collsarn eardrums nary burst and my brains was gonna fall out, but that didn't happen on account everything went black.

The next thing I recall is I can't recall nothin' at all! Hoowee, I must've hit somethin' fierce on account I went to spinnin' and didn't have time to do no thinkin' at all. Now here I am and I can't yet figure out where AM is.

I don't right know for sure yet, but somethin' must be off-kilter in the space-time continuum, on account the place I'm writin' this from ain't no place I ought to be.

You see I died twice, and as collsarn looney as it sounds, I went to hell. Oh I got myself out all right, but the how and why reasons of escapin' the clutches of Satan elude me right now.

Today, I am speakin' at you from just beyond the Pearly Gates.

It could be the belly of a whale, but they ain't got no whales in the Everglades, so iffen it was anything it'd be one big bull gator's guts. Best I know gators don't have pearly white teeth, so whatever I got swallowed up by it's already digested me, and ain't pooped me out yet.

Since I've already been to Hades I know where I'm not. This place has a thinkputer, a thingamajig that alls I gotta do is think thoughts and they show up as words floatin' in the air. So bein' the speechifyin' guy I am, this must be heaven!

All those stories, the books, movies, bedtime tales about angels and clouds, and that fluffy stuff. I'll tell you right now it ain't so.

I did piss a lot of folks off in a prior death or two, but that was accidental. I landed in a hospital, was put on life support, and plum declared dead. Hellsfire they'd already called the folks from UNOS to pluck out my organs and implant `em in other folks. That there was a funky time, and whole different story.

So here I am dead again, and I'm in heaven. I can barely believe it myself.

I never thought I'd say those words, but sure enough. Don't tell anyone I snuck in.
I'll tell you about that later. Right now I gotta check things out.

I need to be real careful because there's a real good chance of me gettin' kicked out, maybe banned for all eternity, so I best be polite to everyone. Like treatin' these pasty dead wispy folks like kin-the ones who were sober half the time-or else I'll be in some pickle. Seein' as I've been a guest of Hades a couple times, Ole Mister Mephistopheles'd sure make things rough on my sorry soul, and I've only got one eternity to spend. Collsarn Satan'd have me clippin' toenails in hell's nursing homes. The stink of pee, puke, and ghoulish decay . . . eew, I can't even think about it.

But I CAN think. Um-hmm, I still got free will. I can walk right out those gates any time I want, I think . . . yep, I still got feet on me. Well I'm goin' to use `em and check out the scene up here.

I'll be back at you.

2

Search Party Shenanigans

It's been a while since Eustice disappeared in the Everglades. There was no trace of his remains. Nope, nothing at all. Then again there wasn't much of a search party either. The search and rescue teams concluded that after a month or so, there wasn't much of a chance of Eustice surviving.

The people he rented the airboat from suspected something sinister. Being South Florida stranger things have happened than ripping off an airboat. The owners of the Everglades Airboat Tour Emporium filed an insurance claim knowing they'd get their money back. A more thorough investigation by one of the adjustors might yield some solid results, so the insurance company wouldn't have to pay the claim. This was a lawsuit if Seeney ever popped up, and they knew it. Seeney, if he was alive could claim the vessel was defective. Nobody wanted that. They all wanted their money, either remaining in the insurance company coffers, or replacing the airboat. And if Eustice stole it they wanted to prosecute him to the full extent of the law.

I am the sole heir to Eustice Seeney's estate. There was only his niece, and she wanted nothing to do with it unless there was some cold hard cash. In which case she wanted half. Bitch. I know that because we were married for a spell, and she lives half the globe away in Australia. Good for me. Good for her.

So being a next of kin relation made me privy to the proceedings. My ex-wife is Seeney's niece. She distanced herself from her uncle years ago, and has not spoken to me at all for at least a decade. So there it is. Me, Trip Wiley, heir apparent to Eustice's worldly possessions. Whoopee.

I met with the claims adjustor, Mr. Carl Reddy, at Seeney's lawyer's office on a cloudy day in March. He refused to accept that Eustice was dead, and insisted the case remain open. The airboat was to be retrieved, and Eustice pay the price for his alleged crime.

The attorney, Buddy Lancaster III, did not seem to mind at all. The longer they investigated the less they would find, and that would translate into a nice out-of-court settlement, and a nice death certificate to present to the life insurance company.

3

Eustice Meets His Heaven Guide

Hoowee this place is funky. I got my body and it feels more like a suit of clothes, like it'd be real easy to step out of and strut around. I don't right know how though, so I figure it'd be best to stay put inside myself until I get to figure out how this place works. Lookin' back I sort of get this flippy trippy brain fog, like you get when you wake up from a dream and you can't remember what it was you were dreamin'. Hellsfire, have I had some whoppers of dreams in my time, but for the life of me can't remember `em nary a few seconds after tappin' the last few drops of pee off my johnson.

If this is heaven then bein' here means you get to leave all the crummy thoughts behind. I got a flash of somethin' sayin': "No baggage allowed" in all sorts of different languages when I first got here but didn't pay it no mind.

Oh yeah, there wasn't some old dude with a long white beard askin' to check my ID, and nobody's got no wings. Folks here just sort of float around smilin' as if they're free of any ruckus.

I don't know about this. Sure I feel good, real mellow like a buzz, but it's not a buzz, it's like everything's even, and there's only some good vibes. I don't even know how long I been here, but every second I am I recall less and less about where I used to be. That's makin' me nervous on account I got a lot to remember, and I don't think I ought really be here. I wish I had someone to talk to about this.

"Hello Eustice," This voice says outta no place just as I thought that stuff.

"Howdy, zennybody there?" I ask out loud. I think it's out loud on account my thinker brain ain't attached to my voice box.

"Welcome to Heaven. I'm your personal Concierge Angel."

"What the H E double hockey sticks is this?"

"Yo relax my man, this is a cool place. Let me hip you to what's happenin' here."

I swear it sounded like a colored guy. Negros in Heaven? I don't get it. Would they be called African Angelicans, or some politically correct name? I can't figure if they even got politicians here because they were all in hell.

"Hey what's your name?"

"My name's Spooky, and I've been assigned to show you how things work." And sure enough this black guy in a Rasta lookin' hair thing, shades, and a flowing white robe shows up. He hold out a fist and I bump mine with his.

"Nice to meet you Spooky." That fella sure did look familiar. I couldn't right place when and where I knowed him from, but it'd come back to me. I just gave him my most heavenly smile. "Yep, real nice to meet you too. Do I know you from someplace, or did we cross paths when I was livin'?"

"We sure did." He said it fast and turned so his back was facin' me.

Spooky didn't want to answer my question. I reckon it was against the rules. All these metaphysical places got rules. Hell had `em, so's I reckon this place does too. He waved his hand and motioned for me to follow him through the poofy clouds, that weren't clouds at all.

Hell no, they was imaginations. I learnt that as we moved through `em. This heaven is some cool place, and I was feelin' might good among the eternally salvated saved souls of civilization.

4

PIMPIN' IN HEAVEN

When we was float walkin' there was some kinda beams sprinklin' down. It looked like sun beams only luminous, like them Christmas lights. They gave heaven that holiday look and made me feel right good. I was just about to ask my guide what they was for, if they was for anything but decoration, when Spooky turned around and said:

"Yo Eustice you be the pimpinest there is," the Spooky guy named Spooky said.

"What in tarnation's that s'posed to mean?"

"Pimpin', mon. Pimpin'. Thass when you gots the right clothes in the right place, with the right ho's. Pimpin'. You dig?"

"I ain't no pimp Mr. Angel man. Never was. Never will be. This ain't the heaven them terrorists go to with the virgins and stuff, is it?"

"Say what?"

"You heard me. If this is that aye rab heaven I'd rather go on back to hell."

"Chill man. You is the Mac Daddy my man, and that mean you get the best of the best we got here. Word from the top. The bad guys don't get in here my man, you know dat." He stopped talking for a beat and pointed his finger upwards. "He says so."

"I ain't gettin' it. Would you please speak plain English. That colored talk is outside my neighborhood of brainfusion."

"All right." Just like that, the fella started to talk like a regular guy.

"Okey dokey Spooky. Tell me which heaven this is?"

"You're in the main entry to the infinite realm."

"Okay so why use all them pimp words."

"Eustice, when someone refers to you as the pimpinest, or Mac Daddy it means that you're a good guy. It is considered in some circles to be the uttermost epitome of bein' pimpin'-as in being in the right place at the right time-further 'pimpin' is not attainable. In fact my man, bein' the pimpinest is the highest compliment a white man could receive."

"Okay. That sounds good."

"You did figure out how to beat what's his name twice."

"I sure did," I told him.

"Not a lot of people ever get out of hell. Nosiree Mac Daddy. That is why your reputation around these parts is well known, and you my man, you, are a hero of sorts."

"I don't reckon myself as no kind of hero, but if it means I get decent toilet paper, floss, and a good cable connection that'll do right fine."

"You're too much, dude, way too much. I think you're gonna be stylin' here."

There he went from one accent to another. I couldn't right tell if he was a street thug, gangster, or some high falutin sort talkin' street. There was a lot to learn, and hoowee I was lookin' forward to it."

5

SAINT JOBS

I got to wonderin' about gettin me a position up here as a saint. I hear that you gotta be Beautifacated, or Canonized, or somethin' likc that.

They say that if somebody does three miracles they get sainted. Now that fella told me that I got out of Hades and wrangled Ole Mister Mephistopheles enough that it might be a possibility, so this is probably a halfway decent gig up here in the clouds.

Oh yeah, that thing people have in their head, that Heaven is up in the sky. Nope. It ain't. Heaven is actually right there, where you are. It's in the spaces between the spaces. In fact I could be sittin' right next to you at this very moment!

You probably wonder how this works, so here: There's a whole lot of dimensions in the space-time continuum, but the fact that there's a whole different way to look at it is helpful.

You know how we humans, when we're livin', can only see the colors of the visible spectrum? Can't see with no collsarn X-ray vision, can we" Nope. Or, can hear them silent dog whistles? Hell no. Only audible sounds. C'mon, you know what I mean it's like imaginin' there's letters of the alphabet beyond Z that you can't pronounce. That there is why heaven can't be found on any map. We ain't got the right equipment to find it when we're livin'.

Up in heaven, or I should say sideways in Heaven, it's a place inside and within and all around all the other places. I think it's got something to do with matter and how it doesn't matter here.

F'rinstance, there is no TIME in Heaven. Nope. No clocks, and everything just goes on and on forever. Once you're in heaven-I learned this from the colored guy-you can bip into anyplace in the universe. Yep, I can go back to dinosaur times, and hang out. I can't touch nothin' or talk to anybody on account that'd be against the rules.

There are some folks that can go on back to earth, sort of step out of this space within space-it's got somethin' to do with atoms and subatomic particles-but here, we're all a big ole gush of energy. And like the man said: Energy can't be created or destroyed, here you are. It don't work this way in hell on account in Hades, all the energy has a negative charge. Am I makin' any sense?

Okay. So I'm a this zappy electrostatical mass-well not really a mass-more like an electric current that's got a good charge on it. I can occupy anything at any time, anyplace in the collsarn universe. Go figure. A guy like me in heaven. Now I'd like the gig of goin' back to earth and helpin' folks out, and that there is this job I'm applyin' for. I guess I gotta poke around till I find out how.

I reckon it'd be cool. Besides, these heaven folks are all happy all the time, and they shrugged off all the worldly things on account in heaven you REALLY DO go on forever into a grand collection of energy, and it's a good energy. Most of the dead folk have forgotten their whole lives and basque in all the good old decency of knowin' everything's gonna be all right.

Technically, I was supposed to have forgot everything I did with my life when I was livin'-remember when I told you about that sense you get when you wake up forgettin' your dreams? Well, I didn't-remember that there's EVIL in this Universe and the BIG GUY has some plans for me.

Thing is, I reckon I gotta get remdumecated in the ways of the Grand Scheme.

People here aren't like all here in that regular sort of way they was on earth.

I'll be pokin around, and be back at you soon.

6

Trip's Worldly Ways

Eustice Seeney was declared dead by the authorities, and I was expecting a nice, fat check from the insurance company. That loot would be terrific. In fact that was some scratch I could've used yesterday.

I owed the attorney, Buddy Lancaster III, his fee, and needed to tie up a few more things before spending some of that good green money, and enjoying the finer things life had to offer. After all I had it comin' to me.

Eustice did not, by any means leave this earth-at least not this time-without an estate. When he had the foul ups at resultant "damages" from the lawsuit(s) that killed him. They, the insurance companies got together and paid out a whopping . . . make that staggering sum. Chump change? Hardly. Those times the hospitals fucked up were used as a reminder to young doctors everywhere, that if you fuck up somebody would pay. So there was that money, which was being held in escrow on the way too.

I'd already had it spent whoring around, paying off some old gambling debts in Vegas, and some nice digs. I did have a few goombahs anxious to collect, and have grown fond of my functional knees. So when I knew the money was coming in I called the folks in Vegas and told them we'd square things up. I really wanted all the monkeys off my back. My ex-wife, Eustice Seeney's niece, her too. She still wouldn't let me see my kids, but we'll get to that later. How much later? Next time I make a long distance call to Australia, that's where she lives.

Dare I mention her name? Sure, Effy Jean Seeney Wiley. I don't think it's necessary to tell you that things didn't end well. My joining in with her Uncle Eustice, leaving our home in Australia to return to the land of my birth to battle Satan on Earth? That didn't fly. She had a hard time believing I was leaving her and the twins to help her uncle: "So you're telling me you're leaving Australia to go fight the forces of evil are you?" That was a tough sell, and the day I left our farm near Alice Springs all those years ago brings back the last image of Effy Jean: Long golden hair, a pair of legs that went up to a heavenly body, and smile that could melt the hardest heart. Oh she was a looker, but she also had a temper. All in all, I had a duty, and that was to my patient, Eustice Seeney. He did die-sort of-and his limp body remained on support to harvest organs-during which he claims to, and I believed him, fight the forces of evil traveling in his mental meanderings to the other side.

I didn't believe it at first, but did capitalize on it in some scientific papers and books. Those didn't go over too well with America's scientific and medical communities hence; thrusting me and my sullied reputation out of any meaningful work as a physician. This happened twice, and as hard to believe, Eustice died and went to hell. No bright white lights, hell. He died and went to hell, and I thought I'd cash in on it. I cashed in on his good looking daughter is about all, and a place to lay low in Australia, quitting medicine completely. Effy Jean never treated me the same, and the kids, well they've grown up under the guidance of Effy's new man. A nice guy they say, a farmer, who took over the farm while I gravitated toward America's seedier ways.

I lived in Vegas for a while, gambling, whoring around, and when the money ran dry took up Elvis impersonation gigs, that paid the bills. I was living at a flea bag hotel with some saucy señorita when I got the call that Eustice opened up a business, and that there was a job waiting for me if I wanted to come to Florida. I still don't know how he found me-the best thugs on earth couldn't-but sure enough, I got a gig at the Soul Salvation Center. That place got us both in heaps of trouble, but did pay well. We went on missions to save souls. Damn was that absurd, and for my efforts-mostly placating Eustice-was written into the will, and tasked to carry on his legacy. Yeah right. Enough of the metaphysical world. The only spirits I wanted came in a bottle, and the only bars I wanted to see were outside of law enforcement. Those so-called missions were a real pain in the tookas. Most people didn't want their eternal souls saved. I tried not to think of my own.

So here I am at what remains of the Soul Salvation Center waiting for bank. Serious bank, and some asshole from the insurance isn't too keen on releasing the funds, even though Eustice has been missing for long enough to be declared dead. The adjustor, Carl Ready, refuses to acknowledge the attorney, Buddy Lancaster III's, numerous requests to let go of the benefits. Old Carly boy is intent on fucking with me. If I was inclined to believe in the SSCs credo: No soul left unsaved, I'd swear this rascal was on Satan's payroll. Nah.

In the meantime, I'm going to use that medical ticket I had reinstated, and make my own bank until this thing finally settles. This thing is the investigation of Carl Reddy. Carl's got me tied up in one question or another promising this will all be settled for once and for all, going on a year. Bullshit. The attorney says to just honor Eustice's last will and testament, that I, Trip Wiley, maintain the SSC-which didn't pay dollar one-and wait.

I'm still waiting, but now I've at least been put on an allowance from the Seeney Estate, administered by Attorney Lancaster, and in the crosshairs of Carl Ready, who I believe suspects Eustice's disappearance as a scam. After all it is Florida, and a guy faking his death isn't unheard of. A guy like Eustice, with his record of suing people even more suspicious.'

I just wish people would stop showing up thinking I can do anything to save their eternal souls-Hell, I don't even know what's going to become of mine let alone anyone else's, and I'm sure no example.

For money? Like I said a skimpy allowance, and my medical work. I'm a clinical researcher, and since I don't plan on sticking around when it starts raining money, don't want to start up any doctor patient relationships. Non clinical medicine baby, that's how I roll. At least for now, then its off to parts unknown.

7

HEAVEN'S RAIN:
Hookers, Hoods, and Pimps in Heaven: The Three Rs, and Learnin' the Ropes

Hoowee, this is some place. No wonder nobody's come back to livin' . . . Well maybe some spirits have, but from what I gather there ain't no rhyme or reason for leavin' heaven. I already learnt folks lose their memory of earth life as if they was weak in' from a dream. That'd be cool I reckon, but I still got me some brain worms. Squiggly thoughts, shards of what was, but not the whole collsarn picture. It's sorta like walkin' into a movie halfway through. Iffen you ask around you get a whole lotta shushin'.I reckon I could just let go and be like every other soul here, but I just can't. Maybe it's on account I'm a real restless soul. Maybe it's on account I ain't done with my earthly chores.

I know that if I let the vibe of this place in, you know, sing with the choir and all, you know, goin' with the flow, all'd be wiped from what I was. Hellsfire! That ain't for me. I know it and sure as there's thoughts I'm thinkin', I am most certain there is but somethin' holdin' back that tide from wipin' my place on earth away.

If you let it Heaven's ways wash over you like the collsarn ocean washes on up a beach, erodin' away the footsteps in the sand all day long.

Up here in Heaven them indentations are the days of your life, the memories, troubles, hassles, and the only thing that's left when the tides go out are smooth granules. They's made of energy that are all nice and fuzzy warm. You don't get that longin' to see loved ones, or kin, nope, this is a sense Heaven-folk get that no matter what everything is going to be fine.

There's weather in heaven. Yep. I nary didn't believe it myself, but there'd be some kinda rain every now and then. I din't know what it was or why. But it looked like those Jimmies on a cupcake, you know those sprinkles? They're funky though on account they glow like they're radioactive. I was standin' in a storm just a few beats back and put a few of `em in my pocket. I reckon I could use `em in case I ever get me an appetite.

I learned about that not havin' memory stuff too, in my wanderin' about in Heaven time. I was still waitin' on Spooky, my cosmic concierge, to get back at me about gettin' an angel gig on account I still got a bunch of memories of life, plus I know the ins and outs of Satan's sneaky ways. Personally between me, you, and Boss . . . I don't right think I really belong here.

Spooky appeared out of nowhere just like that CHECK ENGINE LIGHT bips on in your car. And says: "How can I help you?"

"Hey Spooky, do you know if there's a special zone of heaven where all the folks I thought were bad guys hang out? I need some company. Oh yeah, what're them sprinkles of light that show up every now and then?"

"Yes, Eustice, there is a place," he goes and points in a direction, and just like that I'm there in another subdivision of heaven. That was pretty cool the way you just bip around up here.

There it was, the division of heaven for the not-so-bad bad guys. I reckon that's near the hookers with a heart of gold zone too. There was a sign written in some sparkly letters that said: Region of Redeemed Recidivists. That'd be the three R's of heaven.

"Hey Spooky, them sprinkles, you was gonna tell me what that's all about?"

"Those are cosmic karmic juju sprinkles, or CKJS."

"I ain't never seen nothin' like it. What do they do?"

"They're part of heaven's plan. They come in squalls and erase any memories heaven's inhabitants may have of a life on earth."

"That's pretty cool. How come they're not workin' on me?" I asked. Knowin' I had some in my pocket and my thinker brain was rarin' up with thoughts and memories comin' faster and furiousier than ever.

"Don't you be worryin', mon." He said. But I could tell he was worried.

That's when I got my first inclination somethin' was off-kilter. I got me to wonderin' why there ain't never been a rain storm of heavenly weather on earth, but reckoned it was saved for when you got dead.

8

HEAVEN . . . I'M IN HEAVEN (They had better TV in Hades-I heard it was the deception perception)

So I'm up here in Heaven and some guy come over to me and says: "Eustitheh, I beckon you to readeth thyne verse."

I say: "What the hay ell are you talklin' about? Don't you speak no English?"

"Simpleton."

"HEY this here's Heaven and you gotta be nice to people."

"Read." Then he dropped the paper, or whatever it was and just upped and left.

There's things up here in Heaven don't make no sense at all. This page is floatin' around and there's letters that jump up and sort of talk at you. I guess it's for them folks that were blind or somethin' that went to heaven.

"I ain't readin' but for nothin'" I says, and the fella just ups`n walks away all huffy. Fuck em'-Oops

FORHEAVENSTAKE

I don't reckon you can say words like that in Heaven, then again, what're they gonna do to you? You're already collsarn dead.

9

BACK AT THE SOUL SALVATION CENTER

Carl Reddy was in the office. I wasn't sure if he was the sort of guy who didn't wear deodorant, or if he did, it was the wrong kind. He was about five foot ten, buzz cut, black plastic rimmed glasses, and a short sleeve button down collar shirt. He wore a tie with what looked like-and after I found out how he did business-were probably nose picking remnants. He had one of those plastic pocket liners with an assortment of pens, pencils, and markers. Maybe it was the Polyester blend trousers, Clark's shoes, or white socks, something about the guy was just off-kilter.

Why was he at the offices of the Soul Salvation Center?

10

HANGIN' AROUND THE COSMIC CHECK OUT COUNTER
BACK IN HEAVEN AND BORED
(High Fiber and Floatin' Souls)

Hey folks. I gotta tell you that Heaven CAN wait on account I'd like real bad to do somethin' already. That colored guy who'd shown me around said he'd get back at me, but sure's hell, ain't done but for nothin'. I'm impatient I am, and can't stand hangin' around all these peppy spirits floatin' around smilin' and bein' all nicey nice. Heaven? I'd just as soon get goin' doin' somethin' down on earth.

I get to figure that now I got my sea legs I can git goin' on my own. What're they gonna do, kick me outta here?

I got it figured out. When somebody shows up at the check-in counter to get into heaven I can mosey on nearby and find out if they get accepted into this great wonderful foreverness zone. If they don't my guess is they go to that in-between place for reconsideration. Or maybe at least that's what I discovered askin' around-maybe they go to that place called purgatory.

Purgatory, I came to know was a place in between here, Hades, and nothingness. Yep. You can die and just go into the NO ZONE. Sort of like goin' to crash out after a few bottles of Early Times and a few downers.

I happen to know there's a lot of NO ZONE folks who was movie stars, or rock and roll people.

You see I went over to the NO ZONE Floatatorium. Yep that's what the heavensfolk call it, a Floatatorium, or the Floatatorium. (these heaven folks are so polite it's creepy). There's folks there, maybe you heard their records, or seen `em in the movies. They just got bodies hoverin' in space. It'd be spooky, but bein' in heaven and already dead there ain't a whole lot to be afraid of. You see all of us here have been redeemed, whatever that means. I don't feel right redeemed, but we'll get back to that. These floaters I hear can be floatin' for years, maybe centuries. But since there ain't no time here, they just float like a piece high fiber doody in a plugged up toilet. OD'd folk are like high fiber stools in the cosmic crapper.

I was standin' next to some movie star, who'd overdosed on one thing or another, and there she was all pretty, nekkid, and blank. Talk about spending eternity in THAT dopey zone. I reckon when they wake, or if they ever do, they gotta be reckoned with. Word is that Ole Mister Mephistopheles doesn't have first dibs on these folks, the ones who accidentally overdose. So in the

Big Guy's rule book of Heaven, which by the way I didn't really read, these folks are part of Heavens rules. Yep, the in betweeners. I gotta make a note to read that collsarn rule book.

The other part of in-betweeners are the folks who done up and offed themselves. Yep, according to the rule book, if you kill yourself, you get sent to purgatory for a long long spell. I guess you can call it a spell on account that sounds more ethereal, and all a way of the passage of moments. Now them folks, the ones who'd swallowed a bullet, or dove off a bridge on account they didn't want to stick around life, they're in a real pickle of the afterlife.

You see them folks are first in line for Satan's minions to ferret out and drag on over to Hades. I hear they got some options, but there's not a lot. Break the rules, and you get into a bad dead zone.

So that being that, I got to get me on down to earth and make sure my people don't land themselves up in an eternal Heavnation. Yep, that's what goin' to heaven can be. Heaven, can be like Hell in that you're: One. There forever. Two. It can be real crummy. Three. If you follow a few rules while you're livin' you can avoid future crumminess, and then Four. You ain't got no way of knowin' what's in store for you unless your follow the rule book. Yep I gotta get more info on that.

I know I know, it can be perplexin', and there's lots of folks livin' life thinkin' us heavens-people are just happy as clams. Oh yeah, there ain't no clams here. In fact there ain't no animals or nothin' in heaven. Nope, just humans.

Those little old ladies and homeos with the cutesy little foo foo dogs? You know what I mean, they drive around with their pooch and treat it better than they treat themselves? Yep, them folk. If they're lucky and die and get through the cosmic checkout counter and enter heaven they ain't gonna let Poochie in. Cats either. I ain't seen any critters here at all yet, but that fella Spooky, the Negro Angel? He said there'd be some sacred cows here. I'm lookin'

I'm headin' to earth one way or another and settin' folks straight before they die so they don't do some stupid stuff. And give `em the Cliff's Notes of the rules, which I am gonna read right now. That there is a note to mah self.

11

Ridin' the H.E.H. (The Heaven Eleven Highway) GOIN' BACK TO THE WORLD

So I jump off of some puffy thing. Folks'd reckon it'd be a cloud but there ain't no clouds in heaven. I get to fallin' but it ain't fallin' it's travelin'. Hmm . . . Lemme try this: When you leave Heaven you enter this realm or somethin', it ain't like a place you can really imagine because like heaven itself, it's a place that ain't seen by nobody but dead folks.

It's like seein' colors that aren't part of the naturally occurrin' rainbow, like seein' with X-ray vision or somethin'. I can see ultraviolet stuff like them black light posters without no black lightbulb. Your perception sensors is all tweaked. It's like you're in this orchestra and the conductor's up there with that baton ready to set to start wavin' his arms to some classified music you ain't never heard before, and you got a fiddle and can't read music, but can figure it out anyway. Yep. There's some grand conductor here in Heaven that makes things happen just like that.

For me, it's like understandin' some foreign language you ain't never heard, and knowin' what them letters of the alphabet past Z are. Better yet, it's like a gal leavin' a Cartier store without lookin' at the stuff. You're in a whole blotto zone that ain't like nothin' you'll ever see.

So for the sake of tellin' the tale, I'm gonna call this the Heaven Eleven Highway, or HEH for short.

So there I am movin' along the HEH and the first collsarn thing I see is this big ole sign that says: "Caution you are leaving the domain of Heaven with your corporeal body be advised that we are not responsible for any damages or repairs. Please consult with your Heaven Escort."

What the hayell!

And just like that the colored fella, Spooky, shows up. He's right next to me all dressed in street clothes. Fancy ones too. He's got spiffy shades on, Rasta dreadlocks, one of them African shirts-I think they call it a Dashiki or somehtin' like that, slick worn jeans, and the fanciest sportin' shoes I ever done seen.

I gotta tell you this: When I died and went to hell, I got to wonderin' why I was in the body I had during my livin' life. The reason as explained by real live dead people was this: When you die your "energy" or that whole caboodle of electric charge between all your cells remains intact. Some smart guy who done died and got sentenced to hell explained it. In fact, he said the famous inventor

Thomas Edison had tried makin' a device before he died to put his energy into. It was some sort of battery that was the prototype for what they sell at the Sears. I reckon that's why they call it the Die Hard.

Yep, I remember goin' and scopin' out car batteries to see if there was evil or not-so evil spirits hangin out in `em till they called the store police and had me escorted out. But that's a whole different story.

So there I am, travelin down Heaven's Eleven Highway with this fella next to me sayin that he's my escort angel.

"Angel?" I says to him.

"Yes, mon." The guys got an accent too.

"Ziss mean I can't do my thing down on earth unless you're with me?"

"Those are the rules Eustice, can't have you causin' no stir wit de people who're livin out their life, can we?" He points on up toward I know where. I know he means the big guy.

I say: "Yeah, yeah I get it. No sharin' secrets of the afterlife."

"You don't want to be goin' back to Hades, do you mon?"

"HELL NO," I tell him.

"You got to read the rule book too."

"I will I will."

"You do know that you can only spend brief periods of time at any place. You can read people's minds, and you can walk though walls, walk on water, and yes, you can fly. Nobody will be able to see you unless you want to be seen, and you CAN NOT by any means consume any food or beverages."

"Say what Spooky?"

"They will leak right through you. You are, Eustice, one being of pure energy constructed from the interconnections of nerual pathways of your mind, spirit, and soul. You are the embodiment of all you have recalled, developed, and become."

"How bout nooky?"

"Hmm . . . Seeney this is going to be a very vexing journey."

"You tryin' to tell me my johnson's off limits?"

"I am not telling you anything. Just what the limitations may be as you discover them. And, I will be alongside you every step of the way."

"Every step?"

"Yes, every step."

"That could be sorta awkward Spooky. You do know there's places I'm goin' where dark folks ain't welcome?"

"Eustice you weren't paying attention. The only people who'll see us are who we choose to see us. We are, so to speak, ghosts mon. Boo!"

"Hoowee!" That there gave me the heebie jeebies so bad I pert near farted a peanut, but I don't think I had me a collsarn pooper in that corporeal sense that is. You know what I mean? I didn't know for sure iffen I'd have me a regular body sense and all.

"We are just about there Eustice. Are you ready?"

"`Bout as ready as I'll ever be."

That's when it hit me. I knew this dude. He was somethin' in another life, and it wasn't somethin' too nice at all.

"Eustice you are having some unwholesome thoughts. There are memories you should try to leave be."

"You can't stop me from thinkin' what I want," I said. This guy was gettin' me riled so I thunk harder.

Collsarnit, I hate when you can't remember your dreams, but then again that's what happens when you die, most of what you lived becomes just a memory. I reckon the bits and pieces I got, the remnants, will start fillin' in when I get there.

And here goes earth, in that post-mortem heavenly spiritualistic sort of way.

The ghost of Eustice Seeney. Reckon I'll be headed toward some of my old haunts.

12

EARTH AS A DEAD FELLA

So I'm a collsarn ghost. Here I am in my usual and regular haunts, and I'm actually HAUNTING them my collsarn self! Hoowee is that creepy. It'd give me the heebie jeebies if I had any jeebies, but I think they done got put in a state of suspended or full damnation.

I'm here on earth with the specific instructions not to make a ruckus, and remain invisible. I can get people to see me, and listen on up to what I'm sayin' ONLY if I don't spook `em, freak `em out, and I best have somethin' righteous to say, or I get my collsarn spirit whooshed back on up to Heaven to be accounted for.

I don't right know what that means, but my guide this not-so colored, colored guy named Spooky my "angel", who's really a chaperone, is with me every step of the way on my first trip to earth after croakin' and finally gettin' into heaven. That there was a chore, but like Spooky would say:

"Ain't but a ting, mon."

See, the guy can read my mind and say whatever it is I'm gonna say on account I'm dead. I'm in heaven, and no humans are allowed to share the secrets of the afterlife.

It's like I got nuclear secrets or somethin'. Heaven sure ain't what I'd imagined it to be. Nope, no way at all, and personally I'd recommend Hades on account it's a lot more lively. But that's another story, and it's fully splained in other places.

Bein' dead and in Heaven is sorta like bein' in the Aethernet, or the Cloud. I ain't nary but a bundle of charged particles floatin' around foreverness, and sure's hell don't want to be like all those nicey nice unpeople, bippin' around up-well I can't call it "up"-but you know what I mean, in Heaven. Bunch of flaky ghosts.

But the cool position you can get is this whole angel gig, and gettin' to go and hang out on earth is the choice position for any dead person. Truth is most of the other dead folks don't remember nothin' and float around all smiley face wispin' around like birds or somethin'. No harps, wings, or nothin' just this bliss place where you get a choice of not makin' choices. Or you got some remnants left of what or who you was and get called a "restless soul" by the Big Guy.

That's what I reckon I am, so from one restless soul to you livin' folks, look out, I'm back.

"You just better watch what you be doin' mon."

That collsarn Spooky can't get his sorry angel voice outta my head.

So I got my feet on the ground right about where I left this earth, and it sure's lookin' different from it did when I was worried about earthly things. Hell I didn't even have to brush my teeth and floss today.

"Shut up Eustice,"

Sheeyatt. I wish that guy'd shut the fuck up.

"You best be careful what you wish for mon."

All-right, all-right. Can I get on with doin' some good deed now?

"That is what we're here for."

So here we go.

13

MEANWHILE BACK AT THE SOUL SALVATION CENTER

Hey, it's me Trip. I'm sitting here at the SSC staring out the window. It overlooks the parking lot and right now at 2 p.m. it's drizzling. The hookers and dopers are lingering under tattered awnings, and the boarded up shops are just as empty today as they were when my pal Eustice disappeared in the Swamp. Damn is it taking some time for that damn insurance adjustor to settle this case. I really don't know what that douchebag's up to. Waiting for remains? Yeah, right.

It's been a few months since the lawyer, Buddy Lancaster, told me to sit and wait, and that's what I'm doing. I wish I had something to do, but people looking to have guidance about the disposition of their eternal soul really fell into the hands of Seeney.

After all, the guy did die twice, went to hell, and despite people believing it as tommyrot, I believed it. It wasn't because I was his former physician who saw him through both trips to hell either. He did clinically die and was on life support. I was there with him making sure they didn't harvest his organs and dispense with the rest of him. I knew what he'd been though. It's true that he did pay off some gambling debts for me. That got me out of Dodge, Vegas that is, for a while where my life as an Elvis impersonator, whoremonger, and gambler hit a few snags. When Seeney summoned me to join his quest, how could I say no? Yessiree, I was an official soul saver. Yeah, right.

I did all that with Eustice. Now I believed I'd have a lot more "meaning" in my life with the money if I were back in Vegas instead of this bullshit aging office building in Golden Springs, Florida.

A real throwback of urbanization gone wild before the economic collapse and real estate bust of the preteen years of the twenty-first century, but there it is. The modern slum. Maybe slum's too harsh a way to describe the hood. More like a cheapie, white trash, Jerry Springer zone, where everyone's out to make a quick buck.

The plaza the SSC is in, used to be the top of the town center for doctor's offices. Now? Hell, there's a chiropractor next to a take-out Chinese grease pit, and an Oriental nail salon that seems to always be packed. I think there's a tanning salon in there too. Tanning salon in Florida? Yeah, right. More like a quick blow job, wam bam thank you ma'am leave fifty on the counter. Too-da-loo. Oh you need some wipes on the way out? Bleah. The ho's there look like refugees from a John Carpenter slasher flick-AFTER the gory scene.

So I'm sitting at the desk staring at the phone deciding if I should stroll over to the shot and a beer bar in the plaza and join the day drinkers. That's always a thought. Yeah, that's a plan. I stood up, Jeez was my butt numb from sitting, staring at the phone, and moved around. I looked at my reflection in the paper towel dispenser next to the sink. Yeah there was a sink. This used to be a medical office, and me being a doc, sort of made sense that I kept my name on the door. I made sure the sign on the plate glass door, which had the words Soul Salvation Center and Trip Wilcy, MD, had the words NO NEW PATIENTS . . . I think that'd scare off any comers.

The phone rang and I nearly jumped out of my skin. First time today. Best I act busy and let it ring a few times at least till my butt cramp wears off.

"Hello," I said. Glad I was standing up, I always think better on my feet.

"Carl Reddy here."

Great, I thought to myself. The putz was supposed to call Buddy, the friggin' lawyer, not me. What the fuck is this about" Should I be a nice guy, or just blow him off and hit the bar for some serious self-medication? Eh, what the hell.

"Um-hmm," I said. "How can I help you Mr. Reddy?"

There was a long pause and the line went dead. What the fuck?

The lights in the consultation room flickered and went out. Holy shit. It's raining but there's no storm. I look out the window and see the lights are out on the signs at the nail salon, and Chinese take-out joint. Power failure. Shit. I hope the bar's not shut down. The place IS dark, but I know they don't have any lighting other than an old jukebox. I leave the consultation room and head toward the hallway to check things out. Something funky's in the air and I feel edgy. My blood sugar's probably low, I forgot to eat anything today.

Maybe pop in on a neighbor, see if any of them are around. I could grab a few candies, maybe swipe a flashlight from the finicky dentist, Benny Legume.

I'm standing in the waiting room blindly fiddling with all the deadbolts. Five of them. Fucking five Schlage custom spring action dead bolts. Boink, boink, boink the door opened. I hustled on down the hall toward the dentist's office.

That guy's a trip. Benny spent a few years in lockup for killing his fiancé. He got out on a technicality. Freak. Dude spends his off time sniffing laughing gas, nitrous, and playing with Barbie Dolls. Shit if the guy was a Nazi they'd probably be Klaus Barbies. I knock on his door, no answer. The waiting room's empty, what else is new. In this part of town the only people who see dentists are homeys wanting a new grill. Benny, being a bit low on capital works for whatever he can get. I think he uses some 4 karat gold and melts some alloy down, so it looks legit. Cheap bastard freak. Talk about people needing their soul saved. I hope I don't stumble upon him flogging his dolphin with laughing gas strapped on, and a Malibu Barbie in his lap. Shit that'd be a scene. Eh what the fuck there's gotta be a flashlight in this freaks place.

I go from one exam room to the next, finally I see Benny with a plastic face mask on and doll on his lap. Thank whatever powers that be he's not snapping one off. Thank G-d.

"Benny I need a flashlight," I say walking around the room. He's got some battery powered emergency lights on. I rifle through his filthy drawers, Jeez is the place a dump.

"Hep yussef," he says through the plastic inhaler on his face, laughing and fondling his doll.

Finally I find what I'm looking for and click it on to test it. Bingo. I head back to the Soul Salvation Center grabbing a handful of hard candies on the way out.

I was so glad to find a bit of illumination that I didn't pay attention to anything. I missed the man in suede bucks sitting on a chair in the exam room, a valise on his lap.

I would've just merrily went my way back to the consultation room if the guy didn't clear his throat.

"Dr. Wiley," he said.

I stopped. Clicked on the flashlight and aimed it at his face. Son of a whore. It was Carl Reddy. Schmuck.

"How can I help you?"

"I think I'm damned."

I did too, but played dumb. Eustice taught me that much.

"Come on back, we'll talk." I motioned for him to come with me and slid the five dead bolts on home securing the office. Eustice and his fanatic ways must've rubbed off on me.

We walked down the hall past the exam rooms, and past Eusitce's old "secret" chamber." I don't really know what's in there, but when I find the key, and I know I will-I've just been too busy to give a shit-I'll check it out. You never knew with Seeney, maybe he stashed a few bucks in there. I took another look at Reddy, he looked nervous. I offered him one of the candies, he shook his head and murmured a "No thanks," and I chomped down on one and tossed the wrapper on the floor.

"Relax, everything will be fine." I said, knowing it wouldn't be, and not really givin' a shit if the rat bastard died-not here of course-but maybe in the parking lot or something. This fucker was going to hell, fucking insurance prick hell. I think that's next to the stadium of the bad credit souls Eustice used to talk about. Fuck `em. I'll schmooze him enough to get the claim paid, and then back to Vegas.

PART II

THE MISSION

14

There Ain't no WINGS up in Heaven and Eustice Needs Them

It went down like this: Eustice and Spooky show up and see Carl Reddy is REALLY one of Satan's Minions trying to steal Trip's SOUL, and the mission begins.

Hoowee I'm back on terra firma. Feels like firm titties, and right fine at that too. Earth. No smiley faced dead folks. Real live people flimmin' and flammin', walkin' and talkin', bustin' each others balls, fightin', fuckin', and foolin' around like always. Now that's where I right fit in. Maybe I can stir up some ruckus.

"No Eustice." That collsarn colored guy again won't let me have a private thought at all. Oh well.

So, to continue:

We touched down so's I could check in on my life where I left off. Since my rememberin' hasn't been, you know, the best. I DO recall my ole pal Doc Wiley and his heathenistical ways, and that I did leave him my estate. I had me a Soul Salvation Center before I died out in the Everglades. I don't know exactly how, but I do remember Ole Mister Mephistopheles presented me with a dilemma, and I had a choice. I was invited to some sort of cosmic duel. Why was it cosmic? Hellsfire, everything I've done since gettin' dead twice before and comin' back ain't nothin' short of a miracle, right?

Jeez. Whoops, gotta watch what I say. After all, I did meet the fella a few times, but that's a different story, and wouldn't want to piss him off again.

Where was I? Oh yeah. Heck! I went to hell twice, tricked Satan, and started up a Soul Salvage shop to keep people from goin' on over to the dark side,

"Hey mon, none of dat bidness," Spooky was readin' my thoughts again. Ain't no way from gettin' away from a guardian angel, iffen that's what he was. Personally I got to thinkin' he was more like a babysitter.

"Why you gotta keep gettin' in my head, Spooky?" I said.

"It is my duty, Eustice." He said in no uncertain terms, and didn't have no accent either. I reckon he just puts that on as a part of heaven's special effects.

Damn that's hard gettin' used to. Havin' a giant size Rasta lookin' colored guy in a fancy suit-wait a second-now he's wearin' a business suit, looks like a collsarn executive, and I got my old roustabout rags on. Hellsfire, my old Elvis T, flannel shirt, cowboy hat-the straw kind-keeps my hair cool, my favorite jeans and Ostrich skin cowboy boots. Hoowee, I'm ready to rock.

"Don't forget mon, nobody can see you unless you want them to."

"All right all right I get it. I'm a ghost. Boo."

"That's not funny, mon."

"Okay I'll be serious. Can I get a shot and a beer over at the bar before I go over to check up on things?"

"You're dead dummy. First of all, how you gonna pay for it? Then, when the drink falls right through you, it'll look like you peed the bar. How you gonna explain dat? It's in the book Eustice. The Angel Training Manual (ATM) you were supposed to read it if you want to do this."

Blah blah blah. Always some dumbass answer. Heaven's rulebook. Just swell. If the collsarn Creator of the Universe made all this I ought have me a little cash on deposit here, right?

"Yes, that is right, but the rule book says you can't use it until you're familiar with the terrain as a phantom."

"Phantom? That's what I am? I ain't no phantom. I'm just a plain ordinary regular dead guy."

"That came back to life?"

"Well, yes, you did." Spooky seemed like he was contmplatin' his next checkers move.

"Okay Eustice, you're a ghost."

"You're tellin' me that I come back from the dead, as a phantom, which has some pretty crummy connotations, or a ghost, which is just fine with me. But either way a spook with no money in his pockets? I need some loot, and I need it now. I think you're just fussin' with me."

I swear that guardian angel was ready to cattywomp me but good, or crack me over the head, the dead one at that, with his brief case,

"Okay okay, we'll go to the bar and you can find out for yourself. Now make yourself visible. You don't want to just 'show up' out of thin air because that will frighten the earthly ones."

"How the hell am I s'posed to do that?"

"It's in the ATM Eustice."

"There you go with that book again, details details details. I'll just think myself visible."

"Go ahead, mon."

I went into a think. More like a thunk, and bore down real hard like I was gonna drop a deuce on the sidewalk. Uh, uh! I went on like that nary ten minutes. Thought I was gonna poop my guts out only I didn't have any on account I was dead. Then just like that, a snap, crackle, and POP.

There I was starin' at my reflection in this plate glass window. I was of the earth now in a corporeal sort of way. And lookin' I must say, a might spiffy at that too.

The window was some Chinese or Japanese nail salon, and the other image in it was the angel Spooky. I looked down on the sidewalk to make sure there tweren't no turd. Phew. Nothin', that was a relief. I was just wonderin' if there was a peanut in my undies.

"Shut up Eustice."

Blah blah blah. I ought right have bopped him but good, but seein' as how he's the one in charge I just let it pass.

15

Trip's Funky Meeting With Carl Reddy

Trip sat across from the man tapping his left foot. Something about the way the laces of the suede shoes flopped from side to side was hypnotic, or maybe Trip would later recall, simply boring.

"Why do you think you're damned Carl?"

"I sense it." Carl Reddy's voice was pinched and his words enunciated in that-junior high assistant principal caught in the girl's locker room staring through a peephole-way that makes anxiety seem as calm as getting a diagnosis of herpes. "I sensed it since I was assigned this claim."

"Carl, can you be more specific," I asked. Truly not wanting to know more about the putz holding up the claim for Eustice's death benefits.

He said nothing, not a word.

"Does this have anything to do with why you're stalling the claim? Eustice is dead Mr. Reddy. Dead, dead, dead. You insurance people do anything to frustrate benefits, and just enough to ward off any bad-faith claims."

"I would never . . ." Reddy's face tightened like a stomach cramp and his eyes bulged. "Bad faith! How dare you suggest that," he said.

"Relax Reddy, I know you'll make good on the claim. Like any good worker bee you don't want to be responsible for the one that forces my hand, and makes me file a suit. That'd cost your company terrible damages, and make you out as a putz. Hell you may even get demoted if not booted. Maybe you can fetch coffee for the next insurance sap that comes along. Haunted and damned? Hell all insurance adjustors are damned. There's a special place in hell for dickwads like you."

"There's no need for that Mr. Wiley, no need at all. I'm simply doing my job." The eyes settled back along with the rest of him, although a little more comfortable that he'd spewed the party line. He took in a lung full, leaned back, and folded one leg over the other. "About my problem Mr. Wiley . . ." He was as relaxed as a hungry rat in an empty trash bin. "Can you help me?"

Usually I let it slide when someone doesn't use my title, doctor. Shit, I earned the motherfucking title, but why bother correcting him? In most cases I let it slide because most folks are intellectually so unfocused, or multitasking, that vectoring in on any one thing-like a professional designation-could be over their conceptual ceiling as far as attention spans go. But this fucker was a guy who was supposed to be on a case. My friggin case.

He SHOULD know every what, where, and full backstory on me. In fact, he's probably run a background check on me, the claimant, a half dozen times to see if I had any "special qualities" as in a possible scam, which would make his sorry ass job easy. He could just write suspected fraud across the file and say fuck it. Then again he might have looked at it, and saw that Eustice and I go way back. Shit, the records show that I was his doc when he died and came back the first time, and had a publication on the topic to boot. "Interviews with Eustice Seeney," and I did marry Seeney's niece, he'd have to know that too. He'd also know I lost my medical license, probably knew I'd been living in Australia, farming. No way this bullshit insurance company knows what I got in Effy Jean's (that's my ex-wife's name) bank accounts. No way anyone could know where I stashed my worldly debts. Yeah, that's it, he probably did a surface check on my background, the old Lexis Nexis. Saw how shitty my credit was: unpaid bills, debtor suits, casino debt, unpaid bar tabs. Maybe the lawsuit stemming from my unpaid Elvis getups-those sparkly suits weren't cheap-showed up. Son of a bitch.

He was watching me thinking, stroking my sideburns. Still got em. Mutton chops, same Elvis haircut too from the days of his prime, not the fat days when he was all chubbed out. Reddy's studying me like there's some sort of possible angle that's not related to this insurance claim. Maybe he didn't read over the files too closely, and he did have a separate agenda.

I learned something a long time ago. When in doubt regarding human transactions, when you aren't sure what someone's motives are, always apply the: "What's in it for me theory." Maybe there's more in this gig than finding Eustice's remains for Carl Reddy. Maybe, just maybe Carl's looking for his own personal score.

I took a deep breath and let it out slowly, fixed my body language to say I'm cool, calm, and of the relaxed. I'm the driver and you're the passenger, asshole. I laced my fingers together in front of me, raised `em up, and let out the air, placing my hands behind my back, spread my legs in that c'mon buddy show me what you got, I've heard it all before pose, and said: That's Doctor Wiley. Now tell me what you want?"

The cocksucker went white as a friggin' sheet at a Klan rally. He didn't know what to say.

He stared at me staring at him. Damn I was looking every bit the King, very Elvis as ever was, you dig? He seemed to be studying me studying him. There was a long silence and it felt like the room temperature dropped a few degrees. Finally he spoke in a cool even tone:

"I know this is awkward, but I have been having these feelings since I began this investigation. Feelings that I'm . . . I'm going to die miserably. A horrible death. I read your treatise, the books about Seeney's trips to hell. I read them both, and I do know about Eustice. I know how he used his afterlife experience to try and help people. At first I thought it was a clever ploy, a scam to sell books, but there was something that made sense. Awful, terrifying sense. This Soul Salvation Center, he devoted his life to this." Reddy looked around the office and continued. "I started to ask around, priests, clergy, even Hari Krishnas. I never gave it much thought, but now I realize there is a hell. I know there's a hell with every cell in my body." He paused, and stared into my eyes as if asking my permission to continue.

"Go on," I said. "Talk to me."

"I've been having dreams. Vivid dreams, and I see myself in a place that's described in those damned books! I am in hell every time I go to sleep I dread it. I know it sounds silly, ridiculous, but my wife couldn't take it, and she left me. I put everything I had into going from one clergyman to the next until out of nowhere this case shows up at the offices in Buffalo. Why Buffalo? Why my office? Why did it come across MY desk Dr. Wiley? I never believed in any of this nonsense, but THIS . . . Eustice Seeney, and YOU out of nowhere?"

I snarled in the best Elvis impersonator way I could, and let some air out through my clenched teeth. I gotta tell you the guy was freaked, but it could be a ruse. That rap blew me away, and I sure wouldn't show it. I'd play it his way because it seemed like the right thing to do, and, I just might get this claim paid instead of being jerked around. It made sense at the time, and brought to mind a quote a wise grocery store clerk said when she discovered that Jews had an Angel of Death that visited the homes of the first born on Passover: "Fo' real!" Sure I'd play along. Why not?

I brought my hands down and rested my elbows on my knees, formed a steeple under my chin, and said: "Carl, if you expedite this claim, maybe I can help save your soul, getting you on the road to redemption."

16

Carl Leaves the Consult and Reflects on his Rotten Ways Secrets Secrets Secrets

Carl Reddy walked out of the consultation room relieved in the way someone with diarrhea is relieved after the second of a series of serious shits. He knew he'd be back, it was just a matter of when, and how often, and if he'd be stuck on karma's cosmic crapper for all eternity.

This uncertainty bothered him. He'd been a claims adjustor for a long time, and something that was a constant for him. He knew, trained for, went to company outings to pick up new tricks, to deny claims with a smile for. The whole no, no, no, gig with a smile was Carl's claim to a corporate climb up the greasy ladder mantra. His motto was this: All claims are bogus, and all claimants crooks. Always screw the customer before they can screw the company.

Carl had the awareness that he knew what he was doing, and that it was on some level, wrong. Yet chose to proceed, even excel at making people's lives miserable. That is the pivotal predicament that cooks you, and Carl Reddy knew that his time was not long on this earth. A small detail he reflected on as he stood in the waiting room staring at the pebble glass window where a receptionist may have been in the office's heyday as a medical facility.

Maybe, he thought he should have told Wiley that he knew he was dying. He felt that emptiness he'd felt that day up in Buffalo when he sat across from the doctor. What started as what Carl thought was a minor chest cold, revealed to be cancer that had spread. Surgery, as the doctor explained in no uncertain terms, was not an option.

Carl knew that Wiley was a doctor, but couldn't bring himself to reveal the urgency of his affairs that needed to be put in order. There were plenty, and Wiley wasn't the man for any heroic life saving measures. Wiley was the conduit. He just stared at that pebble glass as if it was the pizza faced acne of his first teenage crush both bumpy and clear. Clearly the gal wasn't interested, and hard to see why. Like all opacities his end of life choice weren't going to be very clear at all. He did have the notion that screwing up so many lives by rubber stamping a big CLAIM DENIED across legitimate claims was going to bite him in the ass.

He averted his gaze, scanned the room, and with his lips tightly sealed walked across the waiting room. Saddened that his life had come to this, a last minute plea to the only person he ever heard of who could muster up some defense for his eternal soul. Maybe, he thought to himself it may have been a hasty decision, not like all of the families lives he'd ruined, but one of necessity. A last minute reprieve? He just stood in front of the exit to the hallway wondering how much more awful the chemo would have been. That would have only prolonged his probable life for another month or so. Damn, damn, damn, he reached toward the five locks and in that moment had a crystallization that something had changed so radically in every engram of his person that he was not the same man who came through that door. He had, as if by some divine intervention changed. It was as if the lights suddenly went on in his life.

Actually the lights of the building had come back on, only Carl didn't realize it at the time.

At the moment his hand touched the first of the custom-made Schlage locks his moment not only sparked a chain of events inward, he sensed something, or someone was with him. He looked over his shoulder, maybe Wiley was in the room. No it wasn't Wiley. He felt a presence, and something with a new light shone upon him. It made him uneasy, in fact, Carl Reddy would tell the lady at the bar, was flat out Spooky!

17

Eustice and Spooky at the Bar

I'm finally in a regular sorta place. Hooboy, this gettin' dead, goin' to heaven, meetin' all these flaky braindead morons floatin' around can really be sucky if you catch my drift. Hellsfire, I had some decent times back in Hades, at least the gals was spicy, the bar was hoppin', and I fit right in with all the scofflaws. Now I got this? I'm noddin' my head toward the colored guy they sent along so I wouldn't screw up humans still livin', collsarn rat bastardy weasels. That's Heaven? Sheeyat.

"Eustice we're in the bar.   You got what you wanted, although it is not my place to discipline you, I wish you'd stop thinking those insipid thoughts, they're really beginning to annoy me."

"Annoy you, Spooky? What the hey is you're problem. You're a collsarn angel and've probably seen it all. You can't turn the gears of your thinker brain without some guardian angel gettin' all upside, inside, all the wide way into you're thoughts? Jeez Spooky lighten up and let's get us a brewsky."

So we moseyed on up to the counter and Spookmeister sat down on a barstool. I remained on my feet on account I like to stand when I pour some good hooch down my gullet. I was starin' at my reflection in the mirror. Sure enough I had one, not like in hell where you ain't got no reflection.

The bartender comes on over. A gal in a short skirt with hooters big as cantaloupes and lookin' like they's made of the finest polymer's modernistical science can make, smiles at me. Now that's a sight that'd raise the dead. The gals in hell have their titty implants removed upon arrival and Ole Mister Mephisto forces `em to wear slacks.

"Hi I'm Megan and I'll be servin' you today how can I help you boys?" She says in that sweet cornpone tone, and leans on over to show some of that breastess. A good bar gal knows that move's worth an extra few bucks in tip action.

"Make that a Maker's Mark neat, and two beer chasers Megan,"

She stood up, and shifted her big ole brown eyeballs toward the ceilin' in that rememberin' way folks do when they're not writin' somethin' down, then says: "What's your friend drinking?"

"I think he'll just have a water."

"Water?"

"Yeah, extra tappy."

She leaned forward and put her hand up to her mouth, it's cdgc facing outward and whispered: "Does he have some kinda condition? He does have those dark sunglasses on . . . " She lowered her hand and moved her head around sort of confirming the darkness of the dark shot and a beer bar.

"Naah, he's just fussy."

"Comin' up," she said. I watched her move that fanny toward fine beveragedom.

"Eustice," Spooky said. "I would suggest you keep your comments to yourself."

"Jeez Spooky I was just funnin'."

About two minutes later the drinks are in front of me. Umm-hmm they's lookin' real good. I grab the bourbon, take a big gulp finishin' it, and put it down hard on the Lucite counter and grabbed a beer and chugged it. "Ahh . . . THAT was good," and wiped my mouth with my sleeve.

Spooky was just starin' at his water glass, while I polished off the second beer.

I was just waitin' the thirty seconds till all that booze hits the stomach, and the minute or so till it reaches my brain when Spooky lowers his shades, and the first time I see him smile. Damn that guy had some fancy dental work. Gold shit, a big ole diamond on a front tooth that sparkled just so in the bar's dim light. Now he's laughing. I knew then that somehow I'd met this dude before . . . It'll come back at me. But now he's hasslin' me? I was just about ready to say somethin' to him, when he stands up and excuses him self and says he's gotta go to to the bathroom.

I don't feel but for nothin' at first, and sit there waitin'. While I was waitin' it dawned on me that spooks don't gotta go to the bathroom, and maybe he was up to some otherworldly business. Since time didn't make but for no difference in heaven it sure's hell wouldn't on earth. Next thing I know, Spooky's back beside me.

"That was quick," I said. "Where'd you go?"

He just smiled and said he had to take care of some business. I was just gonna ask him what kind of business when he tossed back that big ole head of dreadlocks and went into a laughin' spell so hard that if I wasn't dead already he'd wake me.

"What the hell's so funny, Spooky?"

"Look at yourself," He says, pointin' at my jeans with one hand and coverin' his mouth with the other. "Look at you."

I look down and all that liquor's on the floor. It's a mess. The bartender, is standin' right next to the puddle. Her hands are clenched up into fists on her hips, and she's shakin' here head. Hooboy. I get to thinkin' I might be in a heapatrouble.

Spooky collected himself and called on out to the barmaid, Megan: "Ma'am, please forgive my friend," Spooky put two one hundred dollar bills on the counter, grabbed my arm just above the elbow and escorted me out of the bar.

"Now can we get on with your mission, right Eustice?"

"All right. all right," I was rubbin' my arm where he grabbed it. They must give these angels some super powers or somethin' cause the place on my arm where he grabbed it really smarted. Damn, hell's lookin' betterer and betterer each moment of bein' dead.

"Okay Spooky let's get on with this." I said. "Any hint about what you got in mind?"

"Let me just say I already sparked the groundwork." He said in that smarty pants know it all way that someone talks when they done dealt from the bottom of the deck.

18

TRIP CARL AND THE ANGELS

I gotta tell you this: Goin' back to my old digs as a spook was collsarn funky. I ain't never been no spook, and pert don't care for it.

"I am beginning to dislike the way you use that term, Eustice," Spooky said. "You are an angel in training. Not a ghost."

Blah blah blah. Okay so that's what I am. Where was I? Yeah, I'm in my good ole body, at my good Ole Soul Salvation Center in Golden Springs Florida, and my good buddy Doc Wiley is runnin' the show. I know he can nary handle the load of salvatin' people on account he ain't never been dead. I ain't no dummy, and neither's Doc WIley. I left him some loot, and my business and all, and hope he don't take to his dark side, gamblin' and whorin' around. That'd be a real cattywompin' to my life work. I did train that boy, took him in as kin when he married my niece. Between me and you: I didn't think it'd work out he's too hedonistical, and Effy? She's a fine young country gal.

Whatever it is, I had to make sure Doc Wiley didn't take to goin' toward the traps Satan laid out.

So we're in the lobby. Me and Spooky that is, and the place looks just like it did when I last seen it. That was when I went to meet them folks out in the Everglades . . . yeah, now it's startin' to come back to me. I was on an airboat. I used to give airboat tours of the swamp when I was a younger fella, so's I know what them gators can do. I reckon I'll find out more about how I died down the road, but ain't no point in the how 'cause dead, is dead, and not goin' to hell for change isn't THAT bad so far.

"You got dat right, mon," my guardian angel has to chime in every one of my collsarn thoughts.

Now it's you're turn to shut the fuck up Spooky, I got to get thinkin' on how I'm goin' to do this.

And just like that we're inside the office, in the waitin' room, like we was transported by Captain Kirk or somethin' I think we're invisible again.

"Yes Eustice. We are. You cannot walk through walls and travel through space in a physical form."

Zat mean I gotts strain like I'm poopin' again to get seen?

"No Eustice. Just like you're taking a deep breath, and bearing down."

"Okey dokey," I say to my escort, chaperone.

"Go and see what Wiley is doing. Tell me what you see. Describe his state of salvation."

"What?"

"Go on, you have a sense you did not have when you were alive."

Hellsfire I did. I didn't even think of it when I was in that bar. That bartender? The one with the cantaloupe boobs, and big brown eyes? I saw somethin' radiate from her. Hell I thought it was just my natural testoasters cookin' up in my johnoson zone.

"No Eustice, you can see people's auras."

Aura? I pert near saw that gal's aureolas. But I saw more on that conrpone cutey, than that. I saw this real shiny glow-I thought it was my eyes and didn't delve much into it on account it bein' so dark in there, but no, it was a real electrical type energy, and I felt it too.

"That's right Eustice your sensory system is tuned to pick up on a soul's disposition. She is a good soul, and will never be enlisted willfully by Satan. He cannot touch her soul. She was an example of an unflawed human."

Now this was confusin' to me. Here's a gal workin' in an almost titty bar, all gussied up, showin' her stuff and all, and she's just fine in the big picture? No hell for her, what the hey?

"No. She is an innocent. A Bopeep if you will."

"Whatever you say, Spooky."

Who's that fella walkin outta the office?

"That is a man who is going to hell." He said it in no uncertain terms, and I could see his aura, and it looked like he had those big ole clamps the police put on your tires iffen you're parked next to a fire hydrant. Yep, this fella was goin' straight to Hades.

19

Carl Reddy Goes to The Bar

Dark as it was, the bar next to the Soul Salvation Center was just what Carl Reddy needed. If there were life-altering events, one of them struck him a few minutes earlier. He felt the jolt on, as if some divine presence said: "Carl clean up your act." Being a non practicing Christian, rather a worshipper at the altar of claim denial, movement up the corporate ladder, and yes, some private little rush from fucking with people, Carl Reddy didn't have much need for bars.

Today, he did. Today, Carl, could never return to the prick persona he'd projected ever again. Those gears that set that mechanism of behavior into play upon responding to a client were selectively clipped away from his psychic transmission, and he couldn't for the life of him get his mind out of the gear he'd been shifted into. By the time he reached the fifth out of the five custom Schlage deadbolts at the SSC, he knew he'd been visited by something supernatural.

Maybe, he thought the miracle that brought him there wasn't really a miracle at all. Maybe it was part of some grander plan, and maybe he thought, that visit to the Center in the guise initially as a claim's adjustor would get him out of the funk he'd been carrying around for the last few months. Or maybe, someone was onto him. Maybe that funky spooky feeling was a warning of sorts that he may be in over his head. Shit. This life has been a real wreck. His wife would be a testament to that.

His wife, Thelma Reddy, had said to him one morning over breakfast, well wait, let me show you:

"Carl, you look horrible," Thelma was woman who by ordinary standards, at least those set by gentlemen from time immemorial was wearing a plaid blue, green, orange, and yellow Polyester blend bathrobe, her hair was in pink curlers, and one of her heavy breasts seemed to want to wander on out for air. It was a full, and at one time many years ago, stimulating breast among the two which Carl at one time enjoyed nuzzling his face between, and humming like a kid in a bathtub making motorboat sounds. It'd been a while since he'd taken a bath-he was a no-nonsense, shit, shower, and shave guy-actually he didn't like to spend much time around mirrors, and too much time in a bathroom could lead to that-nonetheless, it had also been a long time since he'd fancied even fantasizing about bedding Thelma. He thought she'd grown full, frumpy and had hit the proverbial-He guessed it was proverbial because he'd heard the expression, and now lived with it-gal who hit the wall. He was grateful that morning they never had children. He was just wondering where his sex drive had gone when Thelma, placed both hands on her hips, put her cruel thin lips together, and shook her head. Oh no, the bitch is going to sail into me mode. Which it did and she said:

"Carl Reddy. You steamed up the bathroom so much I couldn't put my makeup on and the toilet had a chunk Heaven can only imagine, what in the world could you have eaten last night? Oh who cares, you're supposed to take my car in today and clean it and then pick up my sheet music so I can give my lessons, and . . ."

Carl had already tuned her out, and shoveled spoon after spoon of Cheerios into his mouth. Her voice he would ultimately confess could shrivel a blossoming flower-maybe that's what it did to his cock, but that would be something between him and his urologist. It was time to go to work and get this harridan out of his life for a few hours. Carl Reddy was well aware of why men went off to work, and Thelma put that extra spring in his step, and special zest in rejecting claims. He did have a hate-on for the bitch who'd he witnessed age ten years for each month they'd been married, which would put ten years of marriage into a hundred year sentence of nagging bitch. Damn if he only had the money to leave this wench and her stupid piano lessons. Maybe she'll find some kid prodigy and introduce him to the Buffalo Music Collective and get the fuck out of his life so he could enjoy his down time between fucking with people. Maybe. Then again, Carl considered that morning that if there was a special sort of woman behind every man Thelma, being the shrew she was, he looked at her, standing there yapping. Her lips were moving but there was no sound-like in a movie where the volume's been turned all the way down, she went on and on as the low-fat milk soaked Cheerio's hit his stomach. The wrapped towel on her head highlighted her round chubby face. Boy oh boy, all the makeup in the world wouldn't resurrect whatever it was he once found appealing in her.

Maybe, Carl Reddy thought that day on his way to the office in downtown Buffalo, he had some inkling that he was somehow damned. Maybe hell on earth for Carl was living with this shrew. The Honda started up just fine that day, but something very odd struck him, and stayed with him all the way to the office.

"Sympathy for the Devil" by the Rolling Stones was playing on the car's radio on every channel. Yes. That did send a shiver down his spine, and it very well did make the tiny hairs on his neck stand on end. Every fucking channel for his forty-five minute commute did freak him out, but not any more than the scrawl on the Prelude's windshield still coated with the night's frosty residue. Inscribed was a message: SOUL SALVATION AWAITS. What the fuck? He had pulled the sleeve down on his jacket, a Burberry knockoff Thelma picked up at the flea market and rubbed it off. And then the music, what the fuck was going on?

He considered that day as he sat down at the bar two months later in the dimly lit beer and a shot bar in Golden Springs, Florida drumming his fingers on the Lucite counter. He was staring at the prettiest gal he'd ever set eyes on. Ready to embark upon some day drinking to quell a rising storm of change that by the time he'd slid the fifth deadbolt home, knew was about to occur-and he certainly had to consider what to do next. He watched the bartender, and marveled at her cantaloupe shaped breasts.

"What can I do you for, let me guess, Jack Black and a beer chaser?" She asked knowingly, aiming her gaze at the grim guy.

Carl looked out at her from the catbird caged seat his soul was strapped to. Damn. I can't go back to being a douchebag. I'm going to hell. Shit I have to do something about this. Look at this woman. He said: "Yeah, make it a double."

"Comin' right up." She curtsied, spun around, and had a shot glass, in front of him before he could get the next stream of consciousness going.

"Thanks," he said, marveling at her voice. She spoke in that not-quite murky drawl, and her perky pleasantry grabbed his attention the way Thelma's let it go.

He gunned his drink, and held up the shot glass for another.

"Comin' up sugah," she placed a frosty beer mug down in front of him, smiled, and said: "Ya'all enjoy yourself," and hurried off to tend to the other day drinkers, but not before refilling his shot glass.

Sheesh. This was so unCarl. But so was what happened in Trip Wiley's waiting room.

Something had changed for Carl Reddy, what it was, wasn't exactly clear, but, as he sipped the beer he sensed something would fall into place. He stared at the bartenders butt, and marveled at its architecture, lulled by the warmth of the booze and the syrupy sweet tone of whatever the gal's name was when he felt something tap on his left shoulder.

He turned slowly, and staring him in the face was the second jolt he'd had today, he was looking a dead person square in face.

20

Eustice Tries Rapping With Living folks

Hellsfire! Ain't you hearin' me Trip? I felt like I was in some bubble that wouldn't pop with a big schvartza. What the Sam Hill is goin' on here I'm s'pposed to save this fella?

There I was standin' in my very own office chamber lookin' over Ole Doc Wiley's hippy headed hair on over at a screen. I couldn't believe it . . . Holy Smoke!

I pert near blew a gasket but since I'm dead, and already had two beers and shot of fine sippin' whiskey leak through me, I'd have to reckon any gaskets'd go kablooey into nothingness, or, all over the floor.

Sheeyat! Trip was lookin' at a computer screen that had pornographicated pictures on `em. I had to study on up what happened to this guy on account he WAS gonna inherit my estate and all.

I reach on over to give him a tappety tap, when some electrificated zap goes through me like a bad batch of Tacos or bottle of Mexican bottled water.

"I told you not to be thinkin' you can interfere with earthly ways, mon."

Collsarn it, that guardian angel is gettin to be a real pain in my tookas.

"Okay, okay, Spooky. I feel like I'm in this stupid sack tryin' to punch out of the lining so's I can get some work done."

"Eustice," Spooky folded his arms across his chest-I could see him, but nobody else could and shook that big ole head from side to side like I done ran his cat over. Hellsfire.

"When you're ready Eustice. When you're ready."

"So what do we do I do now?"

"You wait. Someone will come through the door. Study Wiley. See if you see what I see."

I didn't right know what he was talkin' about so leaned on back against the fine genuine artificial laminated panelling I got installed from a couple AA ex-winos workin' at the Home Depot. The put it in on the cheap on account they was both sinners and wanted me to tell 'em how to be saved. I tole 'em flat out that them meetin's was a little hooteedo for

Ole Mister Mephistopheles to hang out and just pluck drunkards all hopped up on coffee and cigarettes. Yep, Lucifer said that he'd get them all dead a might faster iffen they kept goin' to them meetin's and smokin' away.

Back to the business at hand. I got me to lookin' at those pornographical pictures and movies. They was all the same. Some fella put his johnson in some gals womanly place, and the same music blastin' away as if some disco band was playin full time. I'd have to reckon that the music would stick like some ear worm in persons head and lodge there all day after a few hours of porno watchin'. It got to be like watchin' the nature channel. In and out, and in and out, and then squirt , splat, squirt, splat, squirt, splat, and cut to balck. Folks looked like little bugs. Humans sexin' it up on the internet. I reckon Doc Wiley got a kick out of it on account he did some serious studyin', Although, I didn't see him take no notes. He just looked hypnotized by it all.

I don't rightly know how much time went by, heaven not allowin' no clocks or nothin', but it was a spell, till the phone rang. Must've been a good twenty movie clips of gals with more miles on their coozers than the tires on my old truck, and fellas who's pie yoonises stickin' up there like a locked and loaded fifty caliber machine gun under an Apache helicopter vectorin' in on a bush full of terrorists. Only thing was that most of the gals didn't have no pelt in their netherly regions, just lots and lots of tattoos in Chinese, which Spooky told me said all sorts of banal, and mundane things. In fact, there was one gal in the porno movies who must've been some muckety muck pornster that she was in a lot of scenes. She bad a tattoo on her tush that was a big ole scrawl of Oriental letters that Spooky translated. The characters spelled out said: KICK ME. And the fellas? They had plenty of tattoos too, but Spooky said they all said the same thing: "I'm a douchebag." He said that tattoos was a way to separate the real dummies from the ones who wanted first dibs on bein' scanned by Hell's intake folks.

The phone rang, and Wiley picked it up and said hello. I moved forward to see if I could hear who was on the line, but by the time I got there, it ain't that easy rushin' to do somethin' when there ain't no time, he'd already hung up. I did hear him say he'd see `em in a few minutes."

Spooky just broke out in a big ole grin, he flashed a smile, that diamond sparklin' away, and said: "Watch and learn."

21

Carl, Meet Ellen, Ellen . . . You Already Know Carl

The person standing next to Carl Reddy was an attractive, elegant woman with dirty blonde hair, who had the face of woman who's face may have graced any number of fashion magazines. Carl knew that, and he also knew that he investigated her life insurance policy for any funny business years ago. In fact he knew for sure she was dead, and the five million dollar claim was paid out to her next of kin. What the devil is she doing here, now?

"Hello Carl." She said not so much by way of a greeting than as a taunt. "I see you've come to visit a mutual friend.

Did this bitch fake her own death, and scam the company? He finished his beer.

"Go on, have another it's on me." The fancy lady said.

"You're de de de dead, Ellen." Carl said in a no-nonsense tone. "Dammit I saw it myself, you're corpse, you're suicide note. Dammit. I can't let you . . ." He started to stand.

"You can and you will," she shoved him back onto the barstool.

Where the fuck did she get the strength-like a fucking weightlifter-she had an aura about her that her mass was far more dense than his own, the Lucite bar, or anything of this world. Shit, maybe she isn't.

"No, Carl. I'm not. And I do know what you're thinking." You are damned, now lets see how you plan on fixing that."

"Ellen Cahill." He said. "It is you." Carl Reddy saw that his double Jack was planted my sugar lips who'd come and gone without comment leaving his beverage, He gunned it.

"I guess you know all about this, don't you."

"This being you're looking for some way of changing the course of things?"

"How could you know," Carl wiped his sweaty upper lip.

"Because, Carl, I am your guardian angel." She held out her long slender hand with an impossibly thin wrist. Carl thought it looked like some space alien's arm and body alike. So small, and delicate, but powerful."

"Lady I don't know who you're trying to kid, but you aren't Ellen Cahill," he was buzzing.

"Really," she said, and waved her hand.

Everything cut to black. At first Carl thought he detached both retinas, but then he felt himself floating, and something in his guts welled up and he tasted bile. Blind, sick, and floating, SHIT.

He almost wished he was back home with Thelma.

22

EUSTICE GETS CORPOREAL,
Does That Include Dental?

Collsarn if this whole world ain't but for one big ole
testin' grounds set up to challenge folks to find out if
their ripe pickin' for some eternity. Yeah eternity
can be one big batch of zipped outedness where alls
you do is stare off and float around. Seein' as how I
only been to Heaven for a short spell, I know it ain't
the rightful place for me. All this fidgettin' around
and gradually loosin' what's left in mah mind's eye
as each moment of bein' dead rolls by is crummy. I
dug life, even the crummiest parts of it. Dyin' means
leavin' all you ever knew behind and movin' on into
a new dimension where none of that stuff on earth
matters to you-I reckon that it can be all well and
fine, especially if you didn't cash in your life and live
it till you wore yourself out. Folks who'd done that
get some sort of place in the hereafter and they do
get to hang on to ashes of their life's cosmic bong-
some don't. They're just so . . . well, I have to reckon
collsarn euphoric they spend eternity floatin' around
on some astral plane in a suspended buzzification.

That's what my spirit guide, AKA Spooky says.
He told me that the real goody two shoes folks that

went to heaven are happier than all ideas of bein' content can be. He says the folks who go to heaven ain't got . . .

"They ain't got a ting to worry about. Their life, that veil of tears is lifted, and they have no need, or use for their worldly luggage, or rotten husk of a body. Free from the body's decay, the moods, the ills, the shifting pangs of hunger and despair," the fell colored guy waved his hand in that abracadabra way, and said: "Poof. Welcome to eternal bliss."

Hellsfire, you can have that bliss. The ever presence of mind in Hades kept folks in that dead zone on their toes, and maybe why they said hell was hot on account folks in Hades was always dancin' around so fast lookin' over their shoulders cause Old Mephisto always had some chore for them.

One of the chores folks in Hell had was to go back to earth and tempt people into doin' bad shit. Satan can't just steal your soul. You gotta give it up voluntarily. That's a pretty slick gambit. There's folks in the world who wouldn't ordinarily be tempted to do bad stuff, but these Hell angels, not to be confused with the motorcycle club-them guys is capable of makin' a mess out of heaven if you rub `em the wrong way. But there is, a squad of hell folk Satan picks to send on down to earth to taunt into sinnin'. I reckon I always knew that, and all folks have choice-that whole free will thing. You can choose to do crummy, hell, even evil things. Some folks make a habit of it, and Satan rewards `em real nice, until they get sick, and then they really get cattywomped in misery right before he snatches their cosmic dust, sifts it on up, and puts that negative juju to work in Hades. Them bad vibe laden folks hang out forever as a negative force in this world.

I got me to thinkin'.

"Oh no, Eustice . . . please." Spooky said.

I'm REALLY gettin' peeved this guardian angel is monitorin' mah thinker brain.

Mah theory is that like atoms, the building blocks of everything, there is a proton - the positive energy, and neutron the neutral charged particle, and of course the electrons orbitting the sphere's of our life. We all start off netural, and as life goes on after we poke on through our mamma's cooter hole, them electrons, or negatively charged particles, they start bippin' around us. Some folks just incorporate `em into a part of their lives as they grow on up, but remain neutral all along the way. Others, let them negative charges fuss with their neutrality, and that whole life is one big old series of bein' ping ponged by particles pushin' them into bad, bad, bad zones.

"Tank you, mon. Dat was some astrophysics of the afterlife. Not bad though. Not so great either. Now we have some work to do. Yo still want this gig?"

"Hell yes I do," I tole Spooky. "When can I get to use my body?"

"Soon. When you're ready."

Just how my gonna know when that is? I was thinkin' when just like that I turn into a flesh and blood person like I'd been before.

"Remember, you fuck it up, you don't get it back. And there ain't no insurance plan for de angels, mon."

"Okay, okay," I said. I was juss feelin' mah fingers and toes. Felt right good when the colored guys says: "We gotta get back into the aether."

"What?"

"You'll see. Now that you know how to do it, slip into your body like a glove, you can do it again."

And just like that I go all floaty and all. Mind you that it ain't bad to fly around checkin' things out. But Ole Spookmeister must've had some plans for us. I figure it best to just git with the program.

So there I was watchin' from up top like a motion picture show lookin' down point of view, and HOWEE, the things I seen.

I got a feelin' that there's lots of folks loomin' around in this space between spaces, and it aint' altogether wholesome either. I reckon it's as good a place as any to keep track of earthbound folks bein' in this zone, right?

"Dat is our mission, Eustice."

Spooky said it in no uncertain terms. We were here on earth to reckon with the forces of evil, and judgin' by what little I seen, Satan had a whole lotta influence on the collsarn planet.

23

WILEY'S ENCOUNTER

Something was astir and it wasn't something having to do with the porn he'd been watching, which, incidentally was dull, mechanical, and too well rehearsed. Trip wanted to get back to what he was doing, which at first, was nothing, but Carl Reddy's visit annoyed, and the annoyance ran deep. Stirring something Vegas blotted out. Carly Reddy was up to something, he just couldn't put his mind's eye on it, but it took his mind to places that'd been left be for too long. He considered the claims adjustor: His function was to settle claims, and be done with it, and leave. Scurry on out. This sideswipe to soul saving was blackmail of sorts, or maybe it was total bullshit? He just couldn't tell.

Trip wanted to be out of this armpit of the world, and maybe check back in on things in Alice Springs before hitting Vegas. Here, the Florida Peninsula, was no place to linger too long, either was Australia, but there was business to be wrapped up, and an ex-wife IS serious business especially if there's money involved. The man needed to make bank, and that jerko Reddy was standing between him and getting it. Damn, that bugged him more than the pit bosses, or goon collectors.

Wiley learned first hand through all the life and death, souls, salvation and redemption with Eustice, just how short, life is. Nnot that he didn't appreciate it before all this, he just never reflected much on his own mortality. Always an arms-length issue, always someone else. Something changed in him, he evolved. The man he'd been before all this was a version of himself stuck at another part of life, not what he'd become.

Spirit world and hauntings? He'd consider that shit someone else's nonsense and move on to the next sap. Trip Wiley walked among the warm blooded, the flesh, and the pleasures he can derive. He'd say: Call me selfish, self-indulgent, an irresponsible gambler and womanizer. Call me if you want to knock back a few and roll the dice. No more of this aether venture-no, not Wiley, No. No, no.

However, to collect on Seeney, Trip had to lunge once more into that world. That unspoken terrain that's here around us daily, yet nowhere at all.

The state so-called life, that's after this one. The one where our flesh has as much usefulness as my ex-sister-in-law had for a third tit.

Otherworldliness. Even the word sounds like something out of a hack's mouth. Maybe a Tarot reader, or gypsy hawking a future that's gleaned from the threads on your back, or the ride you drove up in.

He shut the lid on the laptop, kicked my comfy chair back from my desk-pardon me, Eustice's old desk-and had to get out of this place. Enough. Reddy set me off into a funk. I could sit here and ruminate, but that'd do no good. Not one bit at all. I had to find what he needed to get what I wanted.

You see, Wiley lacked the skill set Seeney had. Wiley would be quick to admit he can't-maybe didn't want to-visit the world between worlds. Living in a metaphor, digging, probing, and visiting dead, dying, and damned wasn't my bag.

Trip Wiley stood up and checked his pockets for the car keys, walked on down the hall looking at the crazy art Seeney collected-Bizarre, hideous, and grotesque images from former pre-damned "Heathenistacal rascals" that paid us, in gifts rather than money-After all the Soul Salvation Center couldn't, by law, take money from people. We were a charitable lot-yeah, right.

The Hieronymus Bock images reflected the life I'd come to inhabit, not the windowless world of green velvet crap tables, the sound of slots, and smoky rooms, hushed tones, and calls and anteing up. This was my life now, and I may have the keys, but sure wasn't driving.

The door was still unlocked, and headed to the lot. I didn't mention this, but I had this lingering as if sense that . . . naah, it was just my imagination, but it was there. Someone, or something, was setting he would later recall on his right shoulder, and it wasn't a chip.

He asked everyone and no one: What was it that sat on my mind's cosmic clavicle? A weight, but not of significance-no, more an awareness that there a watcher, a presence that impelled me forward. I tried kidding myself the porn may not have been altogether wholesome, rather an indictment of my life, an inkling of how things would bode poorly if I failed this task . . . Task? How the fuck was I going to even begin to save the eternal soul of stranger whom I couldn't stand the sight of, let alone care to help him in any way at all? But I was pushed, more like tickled by some ghostly feather, haunted-yeah, I had to do this one last deed to settle Eustice Seeney's eternal soul. Shit that took a chunk of mindfulness I didn't have a mind for, but there it was I felt it smiling as I unlocked my nineteen fifty nine Cadillac Coupe deVille and sat down in the fluffy driver's seat, checked my hair in the mirror.

His internal dialogue went like this: I may have been by myself, but I wasn't alone. The outlines of a plan were forming as I turned the key. The Caddy sprang to life, all eight cylinders purred like a pussy and like an equation solved the numbers fell into place. I needed to find a medium, not just an average one, but a full blown, non scam, tosser of the tarot, I needed a conduit to the other side.

I put the Caddy in gear and drove. I had an idea where that blue Neon palm flashed and the words: Fortune Teller beckoned suckers. Madame Tsarina. Yeah, I'd consider in regular times, but not today, this was the real deal.

For the first time in my recollection the problem- saving a soul to get what I wanted required extraordinary measures. The grand sum total of my reality dealt was science, but those things didn't cut it. They didn't apply here not with some ordinary solution to an extraordinary situation. No. Not a complex critical mind, lithesome flake - Eh shit, this is the route. I gunned the Caddy toward THAT part of town, as if I wasn't in already in one.

The presence on my shoulder was as real as anything- It was something that'd hit the cosmic fan and sat there like the heavy crown of the soon to be enthroned with a responsibility so great it could free them from the banal and mundane, and

24

NOT YOUR AVERAGE MEDIUM
Tsarina Kaplitzy: Fortune Teller to the Trailer Park Set

The joint was a stand-alone two room dump wedged between a nail salon and a dying anchor grocery store on the edge of relocating. Madame Tsar's Fortune Telling Emporium had a Neon palm in the window and a sun faded "open" sign dangling in the plate glass tinted window.

The emporium faced east. It was on the side of the road just north of Delray Beach, Florida. The road, US Federal Highway, wove Northward from Miami to Jacksonville, sandwiched between Dixie Highway and the industrial and manufacturing joints, thousands of auto repair dives. Populated with the sort of mechanics who knew just swell how to repair a car . . . fix it just right so you'd be back the next week for a return visit, wondering if the mechanic tweaked a wire or hose, or did something to perk up business.

Swell part of the world. And Federal Highway? That was the grand flea market freeway of Florida's physiology-the major artery ran through the state like a clogged vessel stifles circulation to the heart. There was a burned out Burger King, Wallgreen's

Pharmacy, ABC liquor store hundreds of them interspersed between any and every dump of a rag tag business known to man. Some rightfully unknown, but there they were, lined up in some grandeur of shlock hawking their goods to any sap who'd pull into one of the thousands of run-down strip malls on the avenue of suckers. There were dozens of el-cheapo greasy spoons along with chiropractic clinics, whizz-bang miracle working massage parlor tanning salons, and other grimy hole-in-the wall shlock bars between used car lots.

The cars sold were a lot like the shop owners, in that most of them were wrecks who's sun and salt air weathered look had that worn out frazzle, and both had a lot more miles on them than they'd actually would say. Odometers had a way of being turned back much the way a lot folks bronzed from the sun reset their life's clock with a new set of age, history, and credentials. Many with shellacked hair, dyed dark, and knock-off jewelry. The hucksters of the highway had enough in common to be in a state of perpetual competition, never knowing if the dollar store might be sold to a new rube in the never ending hood. Sure there were a few bubbles of affluence, but the seedy and shameless always managed to nudge their way into on of the strip malls to sell what ordinarily would've been given away for peanuts at a garage sale. Not a nice trip, nosiree.

Wiley had been driving for over an hour looking for the joint. He'd reached the Medium's HQ. He heard of it from a client a the Soul Salvation Center, he would have used a directory, but that would have been useless, on account the addresses were often concealed on the seedier dumps, that kept process servers guessing, and made blending in an easier way to conduct whatever unwholesome business they were doing as long as possible without complaint or notice from John Q.

Plenty of fake dentists hawking discount dentures. More chiropractors than real doctors at an accident scene passing out cards, and plenty of acupuncturists, x-rated bookstores. Jeez, didn't these schmoes realize sex to stare at had gone viral over twenty years ago? A few deluxe mom and pop custom "family" pharmacies that were really pill mill drug stores sat with no sense of shame on the owner's part for any reason but to rope in the suckers. Junkies'd pay cash, and be annuitized until the DEA closed in, which was likely years off. Cheap dope, but a Band-Aid would cost thrice the price if it was a legit joint.

The less fiscally fit burbs along the way had banner ads for crappy beer at double the price as regular stores. A sign that the parasitic owners knew the food stamp populace never wandered far from home, or couldn't-they made for easy pickin's by Korean scam artists, Pakistani convenience store owners, or any number of tattered wholesale whorehouses on the strip. The car lots said it all. Tons of them, all packed with beat up wrecks worth less than the parts alone, but sold as spotless wonders with great sound systems. The cars for sale were a lot like the people, Trip considered, as he drove, hoping he'd avoid having to gas up at one of the crummy service stations. They were all, he knew, selling watered down gas. He looked from side to side at the crap that'd become emblematic of the Florida Peninsula, the superhighway of shlock, US One, the Federal Highway the Feds forgot about. Then again, in this state, he mizewell have been one of the crumbs himself in that `59 Cadillac bloody red rag top. Regardless of the wreck he may have been, he still wasn't ready to be cannibalized for spare parts, at least not yet. Trip wasn't going to be like one of the cars in the crappy lots that not only sold the vehicles but leased them out, wrecks for rent by the week-if they ran that long at all.

Trip Wiley had the notion that the cops were in cahoots with the local merchants to time the stop lights just so, to make drivers look around at the manage of mangey markets, maybe stop in and work on his tan-get a hand job from some run down hooker too old to walk the streets. He was just marveling at the riddle of tanning beds in South Florida when he spotted Madame Tsar's Neon Hand.

He pulled the Caddy into one among many empty parking spots, waited until the canvas top's electric motor stopped whirring, and the thump of a sealed classic car filled his ears. Didn't want any of the marauding street thugs to help themselves to his classic sound collection. Then again, most crooks would just slit the roof open, and steal the whole car. That's why he liked to put his bogus police ID on the dashboard.

Trip was often on high alert, maybe a remnant of awareness from Vegas. You never knew who might try and roll you, make a play for your wallet, or try and sell you some worthless piece of crap you can't refuse. It's real tough to say no when you're staring into the black hole at the end of gun's barrel. Hell no. Trip looked around at the store's surrounding Madame K's Emporium.

The usual dives, dumps, and scam traps. He looked over his shoulder at the Caddy, then up and down the sidewalk. A pair of hooded punks smoking cigarettes and sipping beer. A wino asleep on the sidewalk, his paper sack with the bottle in it clutched to his chest. A lazy whore sitting on a bench fussing with her stockings. And shopping carts all over the place, none of them in the usual useful position, mostly in various states of abandon, their wheels removed, some crushed, or half destroyed from cars speeding off from the anchor store-a weak link in a chain of major grocery stores specializing in three day past the expiration date produce.

"Terrific hood," he said loud enough for anyone to hear, but soft enough not to awake the sleeping drunk. His tone was confident enough that if the punks considered ripping his ride they'd have a guy who might be strapped, or may very well put up a fight. Wiley knew all to well that street punks smoking and drinking didn't have the wind, reflexes, or get up and steal like a trained car thief. Besides, he figured he could take both of them with one behind bchind his back. Trip Wiley, MD, tough guy, psychic customer put his right hand on Tsarina Kaplitzy's door buzzer. Cute touch-make a sucker feel important they had to be buzzed in. He tapped it twice, and judging by how quick she responded figured her not too busy to afford him some time away from her crystal ball gazing.

He opened the door to the little shop, and wind chimes clattered an eerie welcome. Within seconds the magic priestess would appear, and put on the hustle-Trip was ready for that. Another day, another scam. The incense stencher let out a Patchouli scent, probably, he thought to conceal the stink of mold, body odor, and sense of foreboding most of these dumps reeked of.

Who came to these dives other than the truly lost? People who've somehow lost their earthly ways. Desperate people, depraved, desolate, doomed or damned people looking for something they already knew. Trip knew all too well that people mostly feared something deep inside of themselves so much they couldn't bear the notion of it surfacing into their consciousness.

Many of these places sandwiched between State Road A-1-A, the ocean road, and Dixie Highway that paralleled the railroad tracks were just hanging on by the filaments of the spider web of lives they'd woven. Scumbags, Wiley muttered to himself. He reflected on the desperate folks, who lingered on life's fringe, hand to mouth, keeping their dubious endeavor's doors open long enough to get saps in for a visit. When an innocent, maybe a tourist, a visitor from some flyover state, or a truly naive Joe or Jane Doe walked in, it'd be showtime. Proprietor scumbag would give whatever poor sap who'd pass across their threshold the best they had, which was the worst and most foul sales pitch an innocent might buy. People from the straight world, the legit world, naive to world's wicked ways were easy pickin' for the crumbs running these little off-the-beaten path dives, and often left a few bucks lighter, or in debt to someone, or something they never imagined coming. Yep, these scumbags were masters at the con. From charge card fraud, identify theft, to misdirect and grab a bag, for these shopkeepers any ripoff was just an ordinary, and usual part of doing business.

"How can I help you young man? I can tell you what is to be your future," The woman said.

"Yeah, right. Lady, I make my own future," Wiley said it loud but not too loud to be disruptive. There were, after all, "other customers."

Fuckng suckers Wiley muttered to himself, but knew the woman heard him . . . the con artist ho probably was going to play the mind-reading gambit here too. An easy enough con if you see what kind of car someone pulls up in, their jewelry, speech pattern, tone, pitch, cadence. Shit, there were so many tells you can pick up, you can predict if they've got a good hand, or nothing at all. Wiley knew how to spot a bluff at the poker table, and that skill carried over into all his dealings. No sucker's moves for him, nope none whatsoever. Gypsy girl wasn't, he figured, playing with anything but a stacked deck.

But she did have a nice presentation. The look, a great costume right out of central casting, and makeup like a pr.

Something about her . . . the peasant shirt and almond shaped face had a striking look accented by a pair of eyes that would've matched any emeralds he'd ever thought as an eye color-they could've been contacts, but something rang true about those eyes. They were almost transparent, and bore at him as if she could see the back of his skull. They were transparent but looked like they'd seen more than the face they fit into. An exotic Slavic high-cheekbone face, with a tint of tan, a gentle spray of freckles peppering her nose and cheeks that extended down her long, thin neck and looked like flesh wallpaper on her décolletage. And the cleavage out-shined any bosomry he'd seen studying the adult rated sites. Can tits have a mind of their own?

If they did this gal, the Tsarina's tits stood up and said: Look at me but her eyes said keep your eyes off my chest.

She was a contradiction of form. The accent was as phony as the fur on the fuzzy dice hanging from his rearview mirror. But that long dark hair and those striking eyes combined with G-d knows what took him off balance. She saw him see her, and for a moment there was a hint of mutual recognition-an "as if" moment-a chemistry without chemicals, a familiarity that rock, scissors stone, has when science meets song, or a dollop of oil meets water. Just how long would it take until it floated to the surface and set there.

"Can I help you?" She took her hand, a tiny delicate number with long, delicate fingers and an impossibly thin wrist, and tucked a long lock of lustrous hair behind a seashell looking ear that could have been something from the depths of a beautiful sea.

An earring dangled from the ear's lobe, a long bejeweled cylindrical number that had some tiny orange stones he'd never seen before, and couldn't help but ask her:

"Those earrings, they're real nice," he said without inflection even though he was inwardly thinking about what she looked like nude.

"Stop looking at my breasts," her voice sounded like Emery cloth passing over a velvet covered stone. "Now show me your right palm." She said it with authority, as a command not a request, and stared hard into his face.

"Sure," Wiley took his eyes off her breasts to meet her gaze, and held out his right hand, palm facing upward. "Shouldn't we do this sitting down?"

"Shut up, and stop staring at my chest." She said, studying his hand. "I've never seen anything like this," she dropped his hand, took a step back and looked to Wiley like she'd just lost what color she had. Her eye's glared like Kryptonite, and if, Wiley thought, he had super powers, he'd sure as hell be dead.

The gypsy woman inched her way backwards toward a table on which sat a transparent globe. It was a crystal ball of sorts set in a palm shaped housing with metal humanoid fingers lacing around it. The moment her rump bumped the table, the atmosphere in the room shifted. The pressure dropped, and seemed to warp and yaw. The ball emitted a soft humming sound, and began to light up. It filled with blue shards of electric squiggles that danced like mini lightning bolts beneath a disco strobe. The ground began to shake as if the earth shifted on it's axis, and a portal appeared in the center of the room. Both of them froze.

They looked at each other helplessly, gripped by some invisible force that drew them like a phantom lasso toward some uncharted terrain. Like it or not, the were going through that door.

25

MYSTIC DIPSTICK

A gust of icy air blew through the little shop. It came from nowhere and the barometric pressure changed. Wiley's ears popped like a jetliner's pressurized cabin gone sonic in a storm. The floor began to let out a hum that escalated into a rumble, and then it shook. Tsarina K started grabbing chochkees from shelves as if her precious nicknacks were of any value if they were swept up in some cataclysmic cosmic storm . . . The ceiling knockdown started to slough off and the room was snowing plaster, shaking violently, finally Tsarina dropped her load of junk and ran to Wiley's embrace.

"What the hell have you brought me? Who are you?"

Wiley stood his ground on a wobble world writing wildly as if ready to engulf and swallow them both whole. She felt good in his arms but he was too engaged in wondering if this was the last woman he'd EVER hold, the storm within the little shop came not from out doors where the sun still shone, but a chain reaction set off by some mingling of minds and an energy spark that set off a cascade of events that was shattering the earth they were barely able to remain balanced on.

She DID feel right in his arms, firm, yet supple, and he felt her surrender whatever this strange woman with bright green eyes and delicate features had. Whatever was happening was happening wasn't because Wiley brought it to her, but because it was meant to be. As if by some grand design, Trip Wiley set out to get who knew what off his shoulders, and got more than he bargained for.

"Lady, I don't know what's happening, but it is happening and I don't know what the hell it is."

Her head was buried in his chest when the room began to spin. Faster and faster as if they were in the center of a merry-go-round, and the world around them were wooden horses on poles. Tip may have imagined this gal on a stripper pole, but not now. Not through this. There was a shift in the axis of reality.

She notched her head back, her hair streaming in the whooshing winds of the rapidly rotating room, some gyroscopic gypsy generator's gears were shifted, and she somehow must have know it.

He stared into her eyes and saw the outlines of reality fade into a blur, just that oval face, and glowing eyes, streams of luminous locks, and the earrings, the curious colored stones began to emit shards of light that let out tangential beams that engulfed them in some sort of prism, a cage of radiant orange light. It was covering them, holding them, grasping them until the eidetic gondola began to move, raise above the whirling room, lifting through the corporeal world, up to, and beyond the ceiling, and up up and into the sky, higher and higher as if it was attached to some unworldly blimp filled with some spacial, and time defying gravity defying aether. They were above the earth, in a place not of the world, but of a space, a place not part of anything but encompassing everything.

"Where the fuck are we?" Wiley said stroking her hair, wondering if he'd have some radiant glow on his palm, and recalling that he wouldn't care.

"You came here because you have seen the other side, and this is our ride."

How the fuck would she know that?

"Dr. Wiley," she said, spreading her arms in a gesture of introduction to the multicolor panorama behind her, "Trip, this is the astral plane."

26

EUSTICE AND SPOOKY HOVER IN THE AETHER

There I was again outside my collsarn body.

"Hey Spooky how come we're Spooks again?"

"That man, Carl Reddy. There was something I saw in him at the Soul Salvation Center waiting room."

I said: "So what. He's collsarn, soon to be damned, right?"

"Eustice, there is a place in Hades that is much worse than the ordinary terrain. Even Satan himself must stay away."

"Why? Somebody let out a big ole stinker?"

"Not funny, Seeney."

"Okay, okay. I thought I saw every compartment there was in Lucifer's Lagoons, Hades Hotel, and the Stadium's of shitbirds with bad credit, lawyers, chiropractors, the whole shebang of bad folks."

"Eustice, the greatest evil ever to walk the earth are those who have torn the very soul from humanity."

"War criminals and terrorists?"

"Worse. Insurance company people."

Hoowee. I ain't even thought for never they was just dummies doin' their job, but now that Spooky mentioned it, them was some pretty rank and rambunctious rotten rats.

"Eustice, that man visiting Trip, he was behaving as a sheep in the attire of a wolf. When you 'died,' the big insurance company held up paying funds for a life insurance policy. They tried to deny it because they could not find your body."

"Yeah maybe you could hip me to that stuff. I pert forgot flat out what did happen to me."

"We'll get to that. Now it is Doc Wiley who is in peril of falling into the trap of one Carl Reddy. A man who is not merely a damned insurance representative, but is indeed a minion of Satan himself. He is, I could read his aura in the waiting room, one of Satan's 'special' agents, who not only converts those righteous people, but uses them to forward his agenda."

"Agender? What in tarnation's that?"

"Carl Reddy knows he's damned, and to assure a place for him in Satan's Special graces must trick people in ways that you could not imagine."

"Well then, let's get crackin'"

"We already are," Spooky said.

Hoowee, this was one wild ride. We was back in the bar where all that liquor drained outta me lookin' at that insurance man gettin' hammered. He was sittin' next to a gal that I swear I knew. In fact I think I knew her so well we just about was hitched.

"You do know her Eustice. Her name is Ellen. Ellen K. Hall. She goes by the name of Ellen Cahill here on earth. But like me, she is a guardian angel, and she is working."

"Why don't we just go on over and say hi?" I said.

"Eustice, please try not to be a nincompoop. We are invisible. Even the barmaid you pissed off for wetting the floor can't see you. Look in the mirror behind the bar . . ."

I moseyed on up to the bar, and took a look over the rows of bottles. Nope, no reflection in the mirror. I saw that insurance man, and was just about read to say howdy doody to Miss Ellen, when she looks up from her conversation with Carl and smiles at me.

I don't right know for sure, but found out she knew me real well. Ellen K. Hall, or ElKay Hall-alkyhol. I was a regular in Hades. She sees me in the bar, and it's like the old days, only we's both dead, and she's full fledged angel workin' on one of Satan's disciples. Carl Reddy. She puts a finger up to her lips, and turns on back to the soon to be toasted insurance man.

What the hell's goin on?

"Eustice, she is getting the insurance man plastered to the blackout zone so he can be put to rest for a few hours. Then we must find Doc Wiley and disengage him, if it isn't too late from whatever Reddy has done with his sprit vectors."

"Spirit vectors?" I said, wonderin' what in Sam Hill that was all about. I ain't never heard of that stuff.

We was just floatin' around the bar, hoverin' and watchin'. I didn't think Spooky would reveal what that vectory stuff was, so I just watched that insurance twerp pummel one drink after another till he was flat out blotto. Then, and only then, when Carl Reddy was slumped on over did Ellen get off her barstool, and transform.

27

TRIP ON THE ASTRAL PLANE

Tsarina K had me just where I wanted her, and I didn't have a clue where that was. I reckoned, as she said it was on the astral plane. Hell, in Vegas fortune tellers were on every block. Everyone wanted to beat random, but I knew there's no way to beat the odds. In Vegas, like life itself, the deck is stacked. Disease, disaster, destruction, shit, all part of the human condition. Things can be just ducky one day, and in a moment, without warning your world can come crashing down. Anything can happen to anyone at any time. That's why I live with the notion, actually more of an attitude, of: "Fuck it, what's the difference?" And get busy with act of squeezing the last drop out of every moment of life's fruits.

Right now the fruits I wouldn't mind take a squeeze at were on the chest of my escort on the astral plane. I didn't think she'd fancy me copping a feel. Nope, at least not right now.

"Come with me," she said grasping my hand, pulling me somewhere in this land of no land at all.

It was a series of ethereal chambers each filled with a collage of images, none so tangible to have three dimensions . . . I guess that's why they call it other-worldly. That's what it is, an infinite plateau that isn't heaven or hell, rather some permutation of the laws of physics-a thermodynamic hyperbole. Some creation of the Divine that's not within the capacity of our mind to conceptualize.

This place was like the place cave dwellers must have imagined was behind the stars, those sparkling holes in the night must have looked like there was a light shining from behind. A miracle, right?

Maybe scientists, philosophers, or artists will come up with a way to describe this someday. But not today.

There was an urgency in the Tsarina K's tone, and we both knew whatever had to be acted on had to be done fast. But something happened. We were caught in some draft, and taken from wherever we were into some formation of other souls hovering about. What the fuck?

28

EUSTICE GETS A LESSON IN HOKEY SOUL SAVERS

So I'm back in the aether place with my collsarn spirit guide. Oh there's folks here, many of `em what'd be called over on earth "zombies" on account they ain't right dead, and they sure ain't livin'. I gotta reckon these are the crummy folks that ain't welcome in Heaven, and Hell's too populated, or figures they ain't rotten tomato headed enough to be damned-Satan can be real picky.

About that head thing? Plenty of `em-the zombatical ones-they done upped and shot themselves. Yep, they're flyin' around on this plane of in-betweenland like1920s era crop-dusters with too much bug juice on board, flyin' low and lugubrious if you catch my drift. I sure don't want to get to rappin' with any of `em.

"Eustice, look at those phantoms," Spooky says pointin' one of his fingers in some direction.

Hoowee, there's a squadron of some rickety souls hoverin' right nearby like they vectored in on us newbies to their zone. They're all jazzed up and circlin' us like bees. Actually more like flies on a big ole turd pile, but I wasn't gonna say that.

"What's with these crumb bums?" I asked Spooky.

"They're 'soothsayers, fortune tellers, and so-called mediums," he says.

Sheeyat, they look more average than anything else. But they sure are annoyin'. Maybe they ought be swatted, and I get to imaginatin' one big ole fly swatter when outta noplace a giant swatter-not your ordinary Sears swatter-but a gimongous genuine artificial wooden handle, plastic shaft, and nary fifty foot wide mesh business end appears. I think it to get to swattin', and it does. It's like I got control over some character on a video game.

Hoowee, some gypsies are really gettin' cattywomped. They's crashin' down like the Red Barron put a few rounds into their fuselages. I don't right know what the plural word for that tube of an airplane is, but did see a box of Fuselex breakfast cereal at the store. That there reminded me that I ain't been hungry for a spell. Nope not one bit at all since I been dead, and I ain't had to take a pee, or drop a deuce neither. I ought ponder that on account I might be consecrated.

Another few gypsy bees get swatted and then outta no-place at all I see my old pal and assistant who'd plum helped get me free from the clutches of

Satan: It's Trip Wiley, or Doc Wiley if you wanna be formal. He's here, in THIS shit hole of the hereafter. Hellsfire, look at that he's with one them gypsy gals. What they hey?

That boy he ain't never gonna learn when to keep that johnson of his tucked in his undies. I ought say the gal was one fine lookin specimen. Now I had to unthink that swatter on account it'd cattywomp both Doc Wiley AND that fine boobied gal but good.

I got me to wonderin' if we could do some catchin' on up about things in this hibbidy jibbidy netherworld.

"Yes, mon," Spooky said.

I hate this mind readin' sheeyat, but what the hell you gonna do? Dead's crummy sometimes.

"Hey Doc!" I hollered. First collsarn pal I'd seen since dyin'.

29

Bros in Space

"Eustice, it's you." Trip said. He'd broke from the gypsy bee formation and was standin', more like hoverin',right next to me and Spooky. He was with the fine hootered gal, and up close she looked even better than she did flyin' around. Seemed like the rest of the hive moved on.

"Who's the lady?" I asked.

"This is the medium that brought me here." Trip Wiley said. "Her name is . . . Damn I fogot."

"Kay. Tova Kay." She said in no uncertain terms.

"I thought your shop had some title, like Madame Tsarina Kaplitzy something or other?" Trip said.

"That was just to rope in the suckers. Now that we're actually HERE I better drop the facade."

"Hellsfire lady," I said, "I know you can't fool the supernaturalated powers that be." I had to tell her that there weren't no fibbin' on the astral plane.

Now that got me to thinkin'. Maybe some day there'll be some earthly company that offers astral trips and all. Maybe an Astral Airways or somethin' like that . . . Um-hmm, that'd be a right fine tourist thing. It'd sure keep folks from doin' dopey things that'd land 'em Hades. I sure got to hope Ole Mister Mephistopheles ain't already got hisself some big Soul Train Aeroplanes on order. Hmm . . . where was I, Oh yeah Trip and the palm reader.

"So what are you doin' here?" I says.

"It's about somebody tryin' to revive your spirit or something funky on earth Eustice. I don't exactly know, but it has to do with your life insurance claim. The adjustor is giving me some hassles, and says he's damned. His name is Carl something or other."

"Reddy, Carl Reddy," Spooky chimed in. "He is an agent of the Devil himself. He is with Hell's Insurance Division. The greatest threat to all humanity than all the disease, famine, war, and genocide together. He is a member of the foul creeping malodorous, evil of the insurance industry that claim to put you in good hands. And you, Doctor, are being recruited by trickery yourself."

"Me?" Wiley said.

The guardian angel, spirit guide spoke in an even, yet urgent tone: "Carl Reddy may have told you he had an Epiphany because he is unaware of his own role, but as we speak, a new peril will be unleashed upon the earth, and Carl Reddy found the perfect dupe on earth to use." He stared at Trip Wiley.

"Nice to meet you too, Spooky," Trip siad. "Again."

"You know this feilla Doc?" I said.

"Of course I do." Wiley snapped back.

"What the hay?"

"Eustice," Trip hitched his thumb toward the huge black man. "He was on earth when you managed to escape from hell, he posed as a pimp, and drove the getaway car, the Bentley, from the hospital where you were in a coma. Don't you remember?"

Just like that, a spark went off in my thinker brain and I saw it real clear. I had just come out of a coma, and this guy, Spooky, was all dressed up like Superfly drivin' a pink convertible with prostitutes and all. He done drove us on up to this mansion where we met Ellen K. Hall, another guardian angel. Hellsfire. I was startin' to get my thinker brain tuned up like a fine soundin' banjo. Only somethin' wasn't right, and a foul twang kept shootin' from

one side of my skull to the other. Why was this goin'
on? How come my first guardian angel is back along
with the other to reckon with some collsarn
INSURANCE man?

30

AN INSURANCE MAN IN ZANENNA LAND

Carl Reddy awoke with a pain his head and didn't know where the fuck he was. The inside of his mouth had a swollen tongue that stuck to his palate. He could taste the foul remains of rye whiskey and cheap beer.

Damn, I shouldn't have had so many drinks. He tried to raise a hand to massage the achy skull, shit, no dice. He finally got his eyes open. They felt shut so tight a layer of goop formed, and it pained to open `em. The effort alone sent ripples of ache through his skull, damn, where was this place. Agh, there, an eye opened, then the next. It was a room lit with pastels, posters, and paraphernalia of an era he missed. There was a makeshift bar in the room, and the huge pictures of Whoopee Goldberg, Barbara Streisand, and Janis Joplin, and Bette Midler gave him a pang of nausea. Maybe it was the hippy days of Haight-Ashbury, or some other throwback free-this, or that era he was dreaming about, but if this was dream something stunk. It smelled like burning wires. He sniffed and sniffed finally his first and who the fuck knew cranial nerves got the message invoking his gag reflex. He spastically dry heaved two, three, four times, with no spew.

Tied to a chair. Tied to a damn fucking chair. He saw the duct tape, silver fucking tape wrapped around his arms to the wooden seat. More tape around his chest. Shit. What happened? Why? The last thing Carl recalled was sitting in the bar, and the sweet whispers of the woman, not Megan the bartender, she was a younger voiced woman, her breasts came to mind and he felt something else, but it was as if some switch in his mind was tampered with and shut that pathway down. He thought again of his last recollections before blacking out. Blackout. That's what he had. It made sense, blackout drunks were great fuckers to deal with. Carl loved denying claims to blackout drunks, they'd forget about the hassle of checking into it, and wouldn't stand a chance in a legal remedy. But wait, Carl WAS a blacked out man who got drunk. Oh shit, he visited Wiley, he went to the bar, he met a woman, and she kept ordering drink after drink. Her name, that fucking bitch wanted to get me drunk. Dammit what was her name?

"Hello Carl," her voice was like the sound of velvet being dragged over sand paper. That lush throaty syrupy sound of a woman, a real woman with years and curves, and the sort of grit a girl like that frumpy wife of his, Thelma wouldn't recognize let alone be. He had to laugh inwardly because the attraction to the woman was immediate. She was the sort of person you just found compelling, and wanted to be with. You wanted to spend time with her, she was . . .

"Intoxicating Carl." She said. "I know what you're thinking. That smell, it's burning bras." She said.

He wrestled against the restraints. "What do you want from me? Let me out of here. I have work to do. Don't you know who I am?"

"I know exactly who you are, so settle yourself back Carl. Welcome to Scorneo."

"Scorneo, what the fuck is that?" He looked around

"You're in hell, Carl. Or at least a part of it."

"Fuck you, lady. Hell's just a rest stop on the road I'm on. You think I'm REALLY afraid of fucking hell? Hell's nothing compared to my place in this universe."

"You DID lie to Trip Wiley, didn't you asshole? I figured that. I want to know why, and I want to know what you people want with him and Seeney."

"Good luck with that, cookie." He emphasized the pastry and wiggled around in the cocoon of silver tape. "

"You were pretty chatty last night Carl. You bragged about your clever self. You were so proud of how you went to see Wiley, how you stroked him, and cried the blues. It was bullshit, and you laughed about it. Your visit was a ruse to frustrate payment of Eustice Seeney's death benefits, I get that much. What exactly is your game, Reddy?"

"You're a smart one cookie. I have about as much concern about hell as you do about drunk dialing. Who're you going to call next, drunken bitch? By the way, fuck you again."

Carl's attitude needed a tune up.

"My name is Ellen. I don't think you'll be fucking anything Carl Reddy. Not now, not tomorrow, not for a long time. And as far as getting out of here, that will be up to you."

"I'm not dead." He said defiantly and looked around the room. A dumpy adobe hut decorated in cutesy college age female dorm room clutter. Teenybopper relics from decades of dopiness scattered all over. What a dump. He took a deep breath and blew it out. What a fucking dive.

"It might be a dive Carl, but you can call it home."

"Good. I like the smell of the place." He notched his head to the open window. "What the fuck is that?"

That's when he first heard it. The sound was a bisynchronous chorus of wailing women. A million Thelma's blathering in some nonsensical thematic rant. But here, they were.

"You like it don't you Carl, it's a lovely sound."

"Fuck you."

"Listen up Carl. They're calling your name, they want you."

"What is that sound?"

"Those are the sounds of scorned women. This is the valley of the scorned-a part of hell that Satan himself refuses to visit. Scorned women who've gone apeshit in life, died along the way spend eternity whining to each other in women talk-Zanenna talk-for eons, and then the wailing begins. It's a far more mind fucking sound than the sirens Ulysses crew heard drawing them to the Mediterranean Island to listen to as they starved to death. No Carl, you're not on your way to Ithaca, rather a trip to starvation, and a seat at Satan's least favorite table to rot until I DECIDE what to do with you."

"What gives YOU the power to take ME anywhere? Why would Satan let YOU into hell to come and go as you please you fucking whore bitch cunt?"

"Satan and I go back a long way. He owes me, and I owe him. I already earned my wings buddy boy. That's right, I may be the angel of booze, but this isn't some Dionysian Revel-not at all douchebag, it's the sound to drive you mad."

"It's nothing I can't handle. I've got a wife who's blather makes this sound like a Waltz."

"Bitching and moaning Carl. Bitching and moaning. How many people did you make bitch and moan throughout your career?"

"Fuck you lady." He spit out the words so loud they nearly drowned out the wails of Scorneo.

"This is a taste of the hell you've put so many people through."

"But I'm not dead. I know it. This is just a dream a booze induced dream you bitch."

"Last night you were dead enough from the liquor to have your soul extracted-which I did-and bring you to this place."

"Scorneo, whining women, burning bras? What the fu . . .?"

"Carl Reddy. You're an agent of the Insuranosphere. Even Satan doesn't want the likes of you. You're soul is so irredeemable it has no 'value' in the grand scheme of things. The place is a creation of it's own. The Insuranosphere, is a place of hideous fumes that engulfs without engulfing, it answers questions with more questions, and leaves humanity in a lurch."

"What do you know, you're just a fucking drunk" Carl's tone shifted hard and fast.

"I'm on to you. The Devil was too. Your people tried to swap out souls stuck between heaven and hell. Trickery, earthly laws, rancid rules, and rotten schemes. That's your team Carl. I brought you here because you're hip deep in MY BUSINESS AND YOU WON'T SUCCEED." She was right up in his face. Her tiny nose was millimeters from his pasty flesh.

"Why here lady . . . if that's what you are?"

"This is the place for you Carl Reddy. Every now and then Heaven and Hell work together to combat some retch far worse than the depths of Hades."

"I'm tired of this. Let me go. Let me wake up from this stupid ass dream."

"It's not a dream. You're going to spend some time in the world of tortured souls. Listen to their whales, the despair, desperation and revulsion around you."

"Why?" He was trying to get his hands free.

"You're not going anywhere until I know what I need to know and do what I have to do."

"Who, or what are you going to do?"

"I'm Ellen Cahill, some people call me Ellen K. Hall, and I am an envoy of sorts."

"Ellen Cahill, Ellen K. Hall . . . Alcohol."

"Some call me that," she said.

"You're a boozy floozy metaphor."

"In some ways I am. You people from the Insuranosphere have wielded too much weight too long, and now you're mine until you're trickery comes to an end."

"You can't kill me. Metaphors can't do shit."

"I am an avenging angel Reddy and can do whatever I wish to people from your camp if you get involved with our people."

"You're talking about Wiley and Seeney aren't you?" He said it like he was spitting out bad sushi.

"Among other things." She said.

"Wiley's coming over to our side." He said righteously.

"I know you're trying, but you won't succeed. Although he's not an innocent, he doesn't warrant Hades, and certainly not an eternity among the likes of you and your people."

"Ha," Carl laughed mirthlessly, a grin about as genuine as the promise of a used car salesman.

"But you see your own demons in him," she said, walking over to the bar, and set into fixing a jigger of some sort of booze. "Time to retoxify Carl. I want to talk some more."

"Screw you bitch." His head notched after he said it, and Ellen would say that his face looked the way a bellyache feels. Eustice would say he looked like one smelly fart, and because Eustice Seeney and Ellen K. Hall go way back, they would both be amused. However here she was trying to extract information from some jerkoff who's got the mistaken belief that he can keep a secret. Ha. No secrets. "I know how Insuranosphere creeps operate and you aren't operating on me. So buckle up asshole."

31

Plannin' on the Astral Plane

Howdy doody from the astral plane. Hoowee this is really somethin' on account I never thought I'd see my old buddy and doc, Trip Wiley, but sure's water's wet, birds tweet, and assholes is assholes, here I am floatin' among the phantoms, spooks, vapors and who the hell knows on this plane.

"Doc Wiley, tell me this will you? I gotta know, how did I die?"

Now it might've been my imagination but somethin' in Trip's way shifted and he right plum didn't seem to have a straight fast answer. In fact, he looked on over at Spooky, who I remembered was a hoodlum, pimp, thief, and overall con man on earth, who was really MY guardian angel. Go figure.

"Eustice," Trip said. He looked on over at Spooky as if askin' permission and the big colored guy just kept a stone face. Collsarn guy looked like one of them dead presidents on Mount Rushmore or somethin'. He wasn't budgin', nope. Not exactly the pimpin' cool cat who knew how to hot-wire a car, break into a fancy hotel, and get Doc Wiley to give him prescriptions for the drugs. Nope, this was one serious no-nonsense businessman in a no-nonsense mood. I reckon there was some otherworldly rules in heaven, and Spooky was obliged to follow `em. I'd have to reckon that he'd done some pretty righteous stuff in the world to bet that angel gig.

I swear that angel, Spooky looked like he was gonna shit a typhoon.

"Go on, mon. Tell him. Trip went to find a link to the afterlife. Tell him what's not to be known. I know there is nothing I can do to stop you. So go. Go ruin everything. Do it if you must."

"Stop!" Madame Kaplitzy AKA Tova Kay said in a deep voice that sounded like she was hollerin' from the bottom of the barrel.

"Ms. Kay," Trip said. "I sought you out to help me find a link to the spirit world. I found you in a dump, but for whatever reason we're all here, right?"

"Why?" I asked. "Ain't she legit enough?"

"She is a medium, mon." Spooky said. "The ability some livin' people have to jive with the spirit world does exist, but most of them have to be labeled quacks and frauds. It would be dangerous for humans to survive if they KNEW FOR SURE of an afterlife. It would take the mystery away, and there would be no FAITH, no HOPE, NO BELIEF in something greater, and the rules of mankind would shatter, and all earth would fall into chaos."

"Mr. Seeney, Madame Kaplizty said. "You're body was never found because you are not completely dead.

BOOM

I felt like a gimongous hand swooped out of no-place and cattywomped me but good on upside my head. I wasn't dead!

HOLY COLLSARN SHEEYATT.

"Calm down, mon, calm down. This isn't such a big deal Eustice."

My brain's thinkin' and my hands is shakin', and I get to figurin'. And the more I get to figurin' the more stirred up I get. Hells flamin' fandango, that colored, transparent, artificial angel was fibbin' me all along I wasn't never set to be no angel at all. What the hey?

I catch my mind from runnin' off with too many ideas and say to myself: Hang on now. I done gone and went to heaven, so that must mean . . .

"It means Eustice that your body is held somewhere in a state Voodoo priests have used since the times of cavemen. Every civilization has

'SPECIAL PEOPLE' the are the high priests, or holy people. The come in many forms. Some are from the tribes of Native Americans, Brujos Brujas, Gurus in the Far East, you name it, mon. There are 'HOLY' people who can see the afterlife in every culture-not just the afterlife but every form of life in between.

"So why'd I get into heaven?"

"It's complicated Eustice," Spooky said.

"Gimme the Reader's Digest version." I said.

"Eustice you escaped hell twice, and that made you what they call in the spirit world a DOUBLE HEX. That is a miracle in itself, to have survived death, gone to Hades, and left. But to have been killed again, the Big Guy," he pointed one of them long dark fingers up-I don't right know which is up in this whole astral plane thing, but I got the point.

I was a freak of the cosmos. Even worse I got noticed by the Boss. Hellsfire I would've been pleased as puppy with a plate of dog chow just hangin' out at my old business the Soul Salvation Center helpin' floks out. But it didn't go down that way. I got sent to heaven.

"You're the walking dead Eustice. You've had a curse put upon you." Madame K's kettle drum voice barreled out.

"So that means my real flesh and blood body is someplace on the earth?"

"That is correct, Eustice," Spooky said.

"That explains why I had bits and pieces of my memory squiggles, right?"

"Yes." Spooky said. "The reason you came to heaven was that someone took your body and is holding it in an EXISTENTIAL COSMOTIC TRANCE, or what we in the afterlife business refer to as the old ECTO state, not a pretty sight, mon. No no no. You're body can be kept alive while your soul floats around forever."

"Hoowee! Why'd anyone wanna do that to me?"

"You are a valuable source of information about hell and now, heaven. We, those of us in heaven, could not let you go to those people who occupy that space between life and death, and control the dealings of an afterlife far worse than hell." Spooky lost whatever accent he had, and I swear that guy sounded like a politician with ten votes shy of winnin' the race.

"What's worse than hell?" I said. Rememberin' that hell was crummy, but I did meet a lot of cool folks there. The food stank, but Satan was jazzin' it up. In fact, last time I was in hell it was lookin' like a nice resort. But I knew when I was in hell that it tweren't that swell of a place to spend eternity. The folks were mean, the water tasted like sulfur, and the air, yeah, yeah, there's some sort of fumes there and it smells like the worst fart imaginable. Hell was crummy, and heaven . . . Like I said you lose all memories of your life and bliss out forever.

That there is when I got the notion that on account I was once the pawn of Satan, I was someone or somethin' else's pawn, and in this big ole chess game of the cosmos, I was bein' moved about the board because there was somethn' worser and worser than gettin' dead and goin' to hell.

"That's right Eustice, heaven called for you to find the CONDUIT."

"What's that?" I asked. I gotta tell you this. I WAS a might angry on account I reckoned I earned gettin' my self right so I'd go to heaven as my just reward. But it was lookin' more like I was bein' used. Not enough a kiss.

Madame K blurted out: "The CONDUIT Eustice is part of an organized system that keeps a soul on hold indefinitely!"

"You mean like a call center to the phone company?" I asked.

"Yes, mon. Only at this call center someone gives you instructions to do one thing or another asking for one thing or another and sends you spinning around never getting a straight answer to send you one way or another. It goes on forever, being in this in-between heaven and hell zone without knowing which way you'll be going. Always providing one more thing that never adds up to being enough. You are held in a state of uncertainty, and no one can claim your soul. The Big Guy, AND Satan are working on fixing this problem." Spooky said.

Trip added: "Sounds like an insurance company."

"It is, mon."

32

Back in Scorneo

"Drink up, Carl. I put a nice straw in your little sippy cup." Ellen said, she was holding a plastic cup under the damned insurance man wondering if the expression that he was just the damned insurance man was too general to describe THIS insurance man.

Carl Reddy, she wondered, the prick shitbird was indeed hellbound. He had something to offer other than the usual insurance company riff about righteously indignant poorly understood company policies, procedures and protocols. But the wondering didn't last long.

"You fucking bitch!" Carl lunged, and head-butted her hard with everything he had.

Damn! The prick connected with that move. His forehead made contact with hers with a clunk she felt into her toes. Not bad for a man tied to a chair. Must have mustered all his strength, and it was surprisingly fierce. The force knocked the drink from her hands and sent all ninety nine pounds of her five foot six frame sprawling.

He shouted: "Hell means nothing to me fool! I won't go to hell I have an eternity of fucking with the likes of you, your so-called angelic friends and the Big Guy himself. Don't you get it you drunk? I AM BEYOND your laws and rules." Reddy was laughing wickedly as he began undoing the restraints and fell back down onto the floor, still partially tied up,

"What the hell," she was splattered in gin, vermouth, and ice cubes. She felt the skin on her forehead for blood, but knew there'd be none-angels don't break that easy, or maybe, just maybe she saw it coming. She dabbed her Anne Klein little black dress with a napkin she'd gotten from the bar and righted herself, walked over to the man in the chair an delivered an open palm wallop to the side of his douchebag face so hard that his duct taped torso quivered, his extremities lurched, and if Doc Wiley was there would have called his response to the slap as a guy waxing up to do a St. Vitus dance.

But dancing wasn't on the mind of Carl Reddy laying flat on his back, knees to the sky, and the absurd posture of a man in a vulnerable position Ellen K. Hall considered giving him an alcohol enema. She paused to consider undoing his trousers, and the thought of touching his privates was enough to make one guardian angel put up her guard. What a putz?

She never made the trip to Scorneo, this wonderful valley on the outskirts of hell without being duly prepared, After all, who could remain mindful with the chit chat of bitchy women whining without needing a drink?

Oddly Carl Reddy didn't seem immune to the wailing ways of Scorneo. In fact he seemed to relish the sound of the canyon's grievous choir.

She contemplated her next move and looked out the window. Ellen had an idea, and it's perfect symmetry filled her mind. It was more of a crystallization of things, a perfect cascade of events she could set in place, and was just about to set them in play as she turned to face Carl, when everything went black.

33

CARL REDDY ESCAPES SCORNEO AND HEADS OFF TO SET THINGS RIGHT WITH HIS BOSS

Reddy managed to squirm out of Ellen's web, bop her on the head with a metal cocktail shaker, and climb out the window into the world of scorned women wailing. At first, he thought the sound would, as Ellen K. Hall said, drive him mad, but it didn't. Carl Reddy, accustomed to the nagging Muumuu clad, hair curler wearing, non-stop yacking face painted ramblings of his miserable wife, Thelma, actually enjoyed the beckoning of the sirens. They wailed, he came to learn, not out of any genuine pain, but because they derived pleasure in it. Carl may have said: Heaven only knows, but didn't have much use for heaven, or for that, hell either. Carl may very well have been in the clutches of Satan, and may very well believed he was headed for eternal damnation, but didn't really care. What he did not tell Doc Wiley, was that it was really just fine to be damned.

Why was it just fine for Carl to be damned for all eternity?

Carl had a trump card, and that was his letter of non-damnation, also known as a LOND. A LOND was an officially stamped-it was a human gut wax melted down seal that was stamped with Satan's signet ring-The Devil's own sign, a Pentagram with some ancient lettering on it. This was a "Get out of hell free," note he'd been granted by his boss whom we'll get to later.

Carl wandered around the valley of the scorned at first not being the most popular of sorts. In fact he was treated much like a zoo animal that'd escaped, and a few scorned gals would have considered tossing a hell net over him, and tossing him into the pit of prison punks. They were the crumbs who'd do all sorts of rotten things to people in jails throughout the world, and being already deemed unredeemable by earth's standards, didn't have a shot at redemption like some of the other prisoners who found some venue to climb out of their prior bad acts funk. But there was no net thrust upon him as he walked through the valley of the shadow of scorned. In fact, he enjoyed the wailing more and more with each grouping of Scornettes. He would later describe Scorneo as a big place where scorned women gathered in groups like they were singing carols on that most revolting day of the year . . . Ew, Christmas. Maybe Yom Kippur too. Carl wasn't big on redemption. His job was, in his life, and that life was to make sure no one living had a chance to get their comeuppance. Carl Reddy was a member of the elite task force of insurance men admitted to the inner sanctum of true believers, TBs.

The TBs existed in a universe onto its own which lie between heaven, hell, earth, and the known universe. It was a was a blip on the space-time continuum that opened every now and then and gave the top insurance executives a glimpse of eternal aggravation. Carl loved the sound of his rubber stamp rejecting claims since the very first days on "the job."

Carl, like many other in the insurance world figured out that the complex labyrinth of insurancedom wasn't merely a business, it was a way of life. Within the industry were many secret societies. Some earth dwellers would compare it to the Masons or Templars, and the truly fanatic would say it was something like the Check Engine Light Society.

No matter how it was portrayed, the secret world of the insurance industry remained shielded by layers upon layers of laws, litigators, and traps, misdirections, politicians, and all the power brokers of the planet, because, after all it was the insurance industry that had all the world's funds, controlled the elections, had the final say on anything humans did on the earth before, and . . . Carl had to chuckle to himself, after life itself.

But this wasn't the time to reflect on HIS place in the universe. This was time to get the boss up to snuff, and find some new way to resolve the issue of Eustice Seeney, Trip Wiley, and the Soul Salvation Center.

The fact that the Big Guy sent an angel to interrogate him, Trip that is, was enough to ratchet up the capture of Trip Wiley, and put an end to Eustice Seeney's little operation to expose the big secret. That was enough to break out the big guns. He needed help getting out of here and needed it quick.

There had to be a crack in the fabric of space and time to eke through to get a message to the Home Office.

Fortunately that day in Scorneo, Wanda Bladletter was struck with a case of post-mortem laryngitis and was laying next to a carcass of a bull. A red one at that. Scorned women had a collective hatred and mistrust of all things masculine, and routine killing of earth bulls was a routine ritual of Scorneo. They'd get a bull tossed over their way by Satan himself once a week to form a circle around and chant curses.

Wanda Bladletter was inhabiting the corporeal body of a nubile nymph rather than the earthly body she owned while alive. That was, as was later revealed several pounds overweight and equipped with hideous dermatological anomalies. Wanda was a bloated psoriatic wench whose husband, the one she took a ball peen hammer to, and bashed his skull in was duly shot six times in the head by Frank Gimbano, an off duty police officer when he chanced upon Wanda in the process of murdering her husband. Hence, her man-hating eternal damnation, and the choice of bodies to occupy in her eternal home in that remote, albeit noisy portion of Hades even Satan couldn't stand.

Rumor had it that Satan had Scorneo on the Multiple Cosmic Listing database, but in the two hundred thousand years it'd been up for sale there was only one potential buyer, and that was an alien life form that wanted the land to drill for sand. NO way, Satan said. Hell, after all, was his domain.

So Wanda, upon meeting the rather droll, and very sneaky Carl was cajoled into assisting him find a means to locate his boss.

The women of Scorneo, as it was explained to Carl, were free to leave Hell for brief periods of time to wander the earth, screaming, whining, and wailing just long enough to piss off a few of the living, but had to return to hell post haste because their corporeal bodies after all, DID belong to Satan. And the Devil reminded the dwellers of the doomed that once you're in hell there's no getting out, unless of course it's on a mission HE decided to send you on.

So, functioning under the assumption that Carl, a man with a LOND letter, was an agent of Satan, agreed to deliver a mission to his boss. After all, if Carl was to leave hell he'd need the help of his boss.

His boss was a man of sorts, rather a force of the supernatural, an ectoplasmic enigma, a phantom of phlebolithic stagnation . . . INSURANNO.

So there it was, Carl found the means to send out a message in a metaphorical body, in the ghostly hell's angel with laryngitis, Wanda Bladletter, murdering wench, man-hater, and soon to be, emissary of the insurance industry.

A gal couldn't ask for a better gig in the universe.

34

Ellen's Quandry

Ellen K. Hall let Carl escape, in fact, Carl HAD TO ESCAPE to let the grand plan's gears shift into place.

She picked up her Astralophone, and rang up the powers that be. She needed to round up Spooky, Eustice, and whoever else she could to set things right. It was true, the universe was off-kilter, and the earth's axis shifted. Heaven, hell, and those in-between zones needed to be set back where they belonged because an intermingling could mean destruction beyond anything ever known.

The Astral-Communicator-Phone, or for short, the Astralophone, shortened among the "in the know" set, to: ACPO, was an ethereal implant of sorts which was granted by "The Big Guy," for certified angels to stay in communication.

So Elen Cahill, AKA Ellen K. Hall, spoke telepathically with Spooky H. Pollack, AKA, from Eustice's point of view, the big black Rasta dude who slipped off to the bathroom when they were at the bar in earth. The very same bar that Ellen took Carl Reddy to and got him drunk off his ass.

There were rules of good and evil and simply drugging him would have been a no no. Alcohol has been around for a long time, and there was no Judeo Christian crime involved. As far as other faiths go, Ellen, Spooky, and many other angels didn't work in that department.

In fact, heaven had so many divisions and subdivisions there were far more than a human mind could conceptualize. Muslims, Taoists, Hari Krishnas, Tribal Deities, even the Ancient Greek and Roman's had their versions of a heaven which in the overall grand scheme of things worked pretty much the same. It went like this: You're born, you life, and you die. If you're life, the one that begins with your first breath of earth air, or in some cases as in Venusians, or some alien world their sustenance become "alive" . . . This is a difficult concept for the so called "Pro-life" people in the twentieth, and twenty-first centuries because humans were not technically "alive" until they consumed a product of "The Big Guy's" creations. So much for that. Are you still with me? Good.

Once you're born into the world-whichever world it is-you are a discrete packet of energy. You are endowed by the Creator with an energy which, as a very bright scientist postulated, and remained an accurate depiction of the fact that energy cannot be created or destroyed. There are atomic and subatomic particles involved, but to simplify the way it works, "the life force" once in existence can't be snuffed out. Oh it can be tampered with, but a human's "aura," if you will can't cease to exist. It'll end up somewhere. That's where the tug of war comes in between Satan and the Originator (another name for the Creator). Satan, wants as much of that life force as he can get hold of to populate hell, and sometimes that energy turns negative. Some scientists have demonstrated that the human body emits an force field of sorts, and that there is an energy, or an aura all human-and some space folks too-have. It can be molded, shaped, bent, twisted, but remember, never destroyed.

Do you know why heaven and hell have been battling? Satan takes advantage of the human's mind, which is pre-programmed, and equipped fully to make choices. Free will. If you make enough negative choices, your energy goes kablooey, and there's this aura of negativity, AKA farshtunken bad vibes, that is easy pickin's for Satan. If you make the right choices, the energy goes positive, and the charge of all those atomic and subatomic particles leaves the body and goes right on up to heaven for all eternity.

Unfortunately there are things on earth that can come between eternal damnation and eternal bliss. That IS exactly what Eustice was dealing with in heaven. All remnants of life as a human revert back to the state of mind a human had in the womb, before they were presented with the choices laid out for them by "The Big Guy." Capish?

You really aren't liable for the thoughts, ideations, actions, behaviors, or anything while you're a fetus in a womb. You're unexposed to G-d's-Or sorry, if you're an atheist, The Big Guy's handiwork.

You see, the Creator of the Universe created mankind in His image, and that image was for humans to ultimately be creative. If you go bonkers by the time of ten, and start into doing bad stuff, that all goes toward your cosmic, karmic score card, and although you have a better shot at redemption, and spinning all those atoms and subatomic particles to a positive energy on down the road, it gets more difficult the more troubles you get involved in.

Humans are given that wonderful gift of redemption, and, as Ellen K. Hall, the temptress of intoxication, when courted casually, respectfully, and not going all dippy and drunk was a decent metric for The Big guy to find out who belongs where and why. Alcohol can, and often does cause those atoms, the protons, neutrons, and electrons spinning wild. Sometime, and Ellen K. will attest to the fact, booze is just an instrument of the The Big Guy. So make no mistake about it, nope Ellen K., wasn't to be taken lightly.

So she called Spooky right away after Carl Reddy, AKA the atom smasher, left his little Q and A in Scorneo.

Satan was kind enough to lend her the the space. After all Carl's employers were beginning to really mess up the simple plan that'd been in place since creation itself. Carl's boss was out of control, and this had to be put to an end.

It was that brief encounter that Spooky had with Carl Reddy as he left Trip Wiley's office unlocking the door. Spooky was with Eustice at the bar when Carl was leaving Wiley. At the moment Carl unlocked the door Spooky appeared momentarily to read through Carl's thoughts, and knew for damn sure if Carl Reddy and his most wicked conniving hangup of man's creations was permitted one human soul an alternative to heaven or hell, or tied up those atoms in such a way that energy couldn't flow freely this could surely mean the end of all things on all planes of reality everywhere in the universe. Eustice still pissed himself and messed up the bar.

Spooky got a fix on a very vile scenario, and a meeting was in order on the astral plane.

Spooky, where are you? Ellen thought hard. Real hard, and she waited until finally, her Astralophone tingled.

Alas, Spooky was with Eustice, Trip Wiley, and someone else. Who else?

Lady Madame Tsarina Kaplitzy. Spooky communicated via the ACPO.

Who the hell is that? Ellen thought.

Spooky communicated that her real name was Tova Kay, a medium.

Ellen had a minor fit . . . a MEDIUM? Those people were like cosmic chiropractors. Dammit, this could really gum up the works.

35

BARBECUED BEANS ON THE ASTRAL PLAIN

So at the time of death, all your worldly ways are just vapors set free from your energy beams. I'm cool with that, but my angel guardians , they wasn't.

We was on one astral plane or another, and I got to hang out with whoever I wanted. I reckoned that I'd done been kilt by my good buddies so they could use me and put an end to the mealy mouth scoundrel Insuranno.

That there is the moment of clarity when all the pieces of whatever puzzle I was in fell into place. I felt a tinglin' like I was gonna pee myself, and got all hibbidy jibbidy. Just then, this big ole hand outta nowhere scoops me up . . .

PART III

THE MEETING

So we was all there on this ionospheric place in nowhere that was in between someplace, yet nowhere at all, and it was all at the same collsarn time!

I have not, nor will I reckon ever get accustomed to travelin' through the space-time, wormhole, whatever, and sure wish I had me some cosmic nausea concoction . . . but hell, that wasn't gonna happen. Who knows, maybe I'd get a chance to hurl on some evildoer? I still had a hankerin' to get things right, and get my ounce of redemption, I never gave up hope. I was just ponderin' that when I felt this hum, like an electric motor or somethin', then that ozone smell made my nose hairs stand on end. The sound got louder, I sneezed, and someone blessed me, and the air upped and whooshed. Then everything started to spark. It was like a bunch of folks started to rub their shoes on a rug and touch a door knob all together, only this was one big rug and one gimongous door knob. I knew then that door opened up into a whole new dimension, one that ain't been seen by nobody from heaven or hell. And just like that the sky, at least I thought it was the sky changed.

There was a huge electrical storm that looked like fireworks goin' off in all different directions. They were so bright I had to shield my eyes, or squint real hard. The colors were mostly blue and purple shootin like comets from this or that direction like a flock of angry, hungry 'buzzards swoopin' in on a carcass.

The scary part was that we were the target of all those shards of astral lightning, that riveted real fierce and let out a sound. It was like some crummy heavy metal band with the biggest and best amps money could buy played by musicians that was tone deaf, or drunk outta their minds. The cosmic cacophony made me wonder if those wailin' women of Scorneo sounded better.

I reckon that explains the way things went down pretty well.

I don't right know how we all was occupyin' the same space without the universe gettin' turned inside out. I say that on account I saw some TV show about things like this: black holes, wormholes, leaks into other dimensions, antimatter, and all kinds of stuff. But this was different in one particular way, and a major one at that:

This was a battle between good and evil with a kicker thrown in. It could be on either side on account there tweren't no tellin' whose side the third player was gonna be in this cosmic game of checkers.

Lot's of folks in the world get to thinkin' and actin' like evil's not so bad, but bad's bad, and if you're doin' evil stuff, thinkin' evil thoughts, you're gonna get a big cattywompin' by the palm of karma. That there is what I reckoned all the insurance buried crats was in for. So I watched, and waited while the trap had been set.

It seemed like every big time insurance company was in cahoots to screw every person on earth alive.

Insurance on earth it turns out was the invention of hoodlums all the many years ago. Some ancient gangsters, probably too lazy to hunt for their own critters, would come around and tell one caveman or another to pay them a dinosaur bone to make sure they were protected from tigers or somethin'.

Cavemen bein' dumb as they were said: "Ugh," which is translated to "Yes," and that there was the beginning of all those agents, claims adjusters, examiners, and all that rot in existence solely to collect stuff from folks, and if there was a catastrophe work on excuses NOT to pay on up for what was covered.

Hell had rules. There was laws, but the Insuranosphere was a place where insurance companies had armies of lawyers who could tie stuff up in one review or another until you lived out your whole life, never seein' a cent from them folks.

Hooboy they's a sneaky bunch them insurance folk. Those rat bastards will do anything to frustrate you. They start with their call centers, their non return of phone call practices and policies, and lots and lots more tricks to keep YOU the consumer from ever gettin' anything you paid for.

I think they called it for what it is in Hades: Indefinite holding pattern perpetrators. Satan couldn't stand dealin' with `em. Nope, not a bit.

They had a fancy place in Hades too, right next to one of the stadiums filled with folks who had bad credit scores on earth, only nicer, and ritzier. They was havin' a good time in hell until they got kicked out. The insurance folks had a grand ballroom of maladjusted adjustors on account there was so many Polyester clothed clerks cluckin' while little bald headed fellas pickin' there noses ran up and down aisles with fake smiles jibbin' and jabbin' the damned messin' up Satan's whole setup.

Finally Satan had it up to his horns, and in the end, when Ole Mister Mephistopheles kicked those suckers out of hell, they formed their own place. I think it was a wormhole into some other dimension hell's team set up to get rid of `em. Collsarn Hades itself didn't want to deal with insurance companies, or the folks who worked for them.

It wasn't some ordinary ethereal zone of heaven or any division of hell whatsoever, it was a hell of it's own creation. A place where you never died, and never really quite lived at all. Stuck between life and death solely to make what existence a soul had uncomfortable. To keep humans, or at least as many as possible in a lurch.

That place was not a creation of man, or the good Lord, the Devil himself shunned it, but knew it existed and had been buildin' up since he kicked them folks out. Like I said: It was not hell nor heaven but a place where dreams were destroyed as if by some giant electromagnet that raises wrecks and drops them in a crusher to squeeze it into a cube to be melted down for whatever metal the market would bear.

Unlike heaven or hell the place didn't want your soul, there was no real "value" in that, no, not at all. The Insuranosphere . . . that was a place the living dead called home. Daily toil to frustrate benefits.

36

INSURANNO

"Ha.," he said it in a tone that'd make the world rumble. Oh he got our attention that's for sure. He went on:

We was all there, but no one said a word, nothin' at all. I think we was all sorta freaked out at first.

"I never lived and most certainly will not die. I was around when the cavemen needed protection from the beasts, the spark that ignited the fires to ward off what terror would come in the dark. I am the shadow that frightens children in their beds. I am the static on the other end of the line that makes you wonder, the glitch in a car's engine, the misfiring weapon in war, the out of synch key in an orchestra's concert. I am what is unexpected. I am what keeps humans awake at night wondering if all the what if this, or what if that, and all the worries combined will come true."

I butted in: "So you're the big Ole Brainworm maker that gets folks to worryin' I said. "Hellsfire I know folks who could drink you under the table and outta their head." I said.

Ellen K blurted out: "No Eustice, those worries and fears come back with a vengeance no matter what people do to numb their minds."

Insuranno continued: "And who would know better but the angel of booze, drugs, and a fools folly than you, Ellen K. Hall. Ha. Tiny foolish humans."

"I am not of the human world," Spooky said.

"No, you aren't and that's why you've got to keep heaven cleansed of OUR POWERS with your silly cosmic rain. That ridiculous rinse that keeps the souls free from the recollections of life."

Hellsfire, that there was the stuff I'd seen when I first got to heaven. That's how come my memory was blankin' on and off. Hmm . . .

"I AM THE grand curator of curiosity and provider of protection that never comes. Ha. Nothing can stop me from being integral to the human psyche!"

"Hell no you can't you collsarn rascally codswallop. I know Satan sure's hell didn't want you in hell on account them folks'd have hope, and . . ."

"Hope Eustice is what keeps us in business. Hope is why Satan NEEDS ME, NEEDS US. Hell couldn't exist without OUR PEOPLE throughout the universe. We're growing and getting stronger daily."

"That's for collsarn sure. You people own ninety percent of humanity, or at least have it insured. You enslaved all humanity for centuries, you rotten rascal.

"You flatter me Eustice, but everyone needs protection, don't they want to sleep at night? I just make sure they don't, and our way is the oft ignored way of mankind."

"No wonder they ain't got a permanent place for you in Hades,"

"And not one in Heaven either, mon." Spooky said as diplomatically as he could. "His people annoy us with their tidbits of this or that silliness that is of no concern to those who are already dead," Spooky said.

Trip Wiley spoke up: "That's right guys, Insruranno is the fly in life's ointment, the entity that selectively saws off the gears of any smooth running machine, be it a chemical reaction, computer glitch, or some unneeded or unwanted thought or ideation."

"Hellsifre he is one hooligan. But you all know that I ain't got nothin' to lose, I done been to heaven and hell, so there's not a lot you can do to me. In fact I done been a plum nuisance to the bunch of you."

Insruanno said: "Don't be silly, I can make you worry. And since the beginning time humans wanted to be free from worry above anything else. I will always be there to raise concerns, make man wonder, and ask himself what if?

"Bullpucky. I tell you. Bull collsarn pucky."

"No worries, mon, he's just tryin' to spring a trap for you."

"Yes Eustice, have a drink and calm down, " Ellen K. Hall said.

Insuranno continued: "You see Seeney without me there would be no heaven or hell. It's me who makes people wonder if they're going to one or the other. It's me who puts the lighting in their dreams.

"Hellsifire Insuranno, you're about to be unscrewed!" I said. That's when the idea in my head went off like the lightbulb in them cartoons.

"Ha. How could an insignificant pest like you stop me?"

"Like this," Eustice said reaching into his pocket, he felt around, finally satisfied and yanked out his hand. He opened his palm, and there was a pile of dust. It glowed like a black light poster in an ultraviolet room. Like the shimmer of a disco light reflecting shards of sparkles on dancing fools.

Ellen and Spooky looked at each other, puzzled at Seeney's concoction.

Eustice took a deep breath and blew the particles at Inaruanno, coating him with a Day-Glo type concoction of paint chips and ash.

Insuranno was covered in cosmic karmic juju sprinkles. He looked himself over and tried, but failed, to flick them off. The longer the sprinkles stuck, the deeper they bore into his being, and the more his memories faded. Right then I could see Insuranno's eternity clock was tickin'. Soon he'd be erased by his own efforts.

You see ain't nobody ever left heaven on account they liked it so much, and heaven's rain, the CKJS was strictly for the purposes of heaven. Me havin' escaped hell, goin' to heaven with a full deck of brain cards, I had me some of that cosmic dust, and plum used it in a way it ain't never been used.

"NOW you big dummy every-time a person gets to worryin' they'll know it ain't but nothin'. I just made a joke outta you Mister Insuranno big shot, and insecurity maker. Try and sell your fear to people now? You're trajectories will all be coated in funny dust, and after puttin' folks on hold, YOU ain't gonna remember but for nothin!"

At that moment the outlines of Insranno's existence became insignificant wisps of dust. The cosmic bolts of lightning ceased, and a calm hung in the air,

Eustice looked at Ellen, Spooky, and Doc Wiley, they remained silent, yet pleased. Collective heaving a heavy sigh of relief.

Finally Spooky said: "Satan's still in business. That means I have my work cut out."

To which Ellen added: "Yes, that's true. I need a drink, you can join me Spooky, after that, I have work too do too."

"Me, I'm going to Vegas for a while." Wiley said. "I need a vacation."

"Hey what about me?" I said.

And just like that, as if nothing had occurred they vanished, as if they never existed at all.

Dénouement

I reckon this is where we're at. The final clarification or resolution of a plot, play or other story. Since this was real life there ain't no smiley face happy snappy stuff. You see, once I found out I tweren't but dead, things fell into place like tumblers on a lock you're tryin' to pick, err, I may have tried pickin' way back when, but that's a different story.

One moment I'm up among the clouds hangin' with the eternal bliss crew in heaven, and next, I'm someplace else. I landed in the midst of a beef between heaven, hell, and smack dab in the in-between space of the universe, and now, I'm revvin' up the engine on my airboat easin' my way out of a thick patch of mangroves.

I open her up, hear the big ole propeller, and see the gators grazin' and know that I'm alive as life can let you be.

I know one thing for certain, and that' this:

If anyone ever is put on hold, and sure's likely will be, it ain't gonna be some toxic cosmic carbuncle set to foulin' up the workin's of heaven and hell. Nope. There may be some rotten scoundrels on earth, and I know they'll all get their due, but at some point in all of everything you can be assured that the insurance folks ain't gonna have a say in the decision makin' process of the universe.